THE BOOKS OF S.

James Lefebure

To P.W –

Thank you for your support & insperation during writing this. You have been a fantastic ally & friend!! And as a great writer I know once said –

Doth The Kraken.

To Terry -

Drop Rock. Death.

(Told you I'd finally finish something.)

First A Warning –

Please be advised
there are trigger warnings for
– abuse, sexual assault, violence, gore,
racial abuse

PROLOGUE - THE BOOK OF ALBERT

Albert had always been a bad boy. Or so he had been told.

"You need to get out," said the Voice.

Albert was ripped from slumber by his father screaming at him from the darkness. He couldn't make out the words, but there was no mistaking the fury in his tone. With a grunt, his father threw a bucket of water over him. Icy fingers dug into Albert's skin. The breath left his body and only panic remained.

Albert had always been a bad boy. Or so he believed.

"You need to get out," the Voice repeated.

Albert barely heard the unknown voice. His body was lost in a sea of confusion and shivers. He knew he was a bad boy. He knew where his soul was heading. Soaking and cold, Albert sat up and gasped for air. In the darkness, his father screamed verse and scripture at him. The words were lost in speed and hate, but the intent was clear.

The second load of water, this time from his mother's bucket, doused him. More freezing hands ran across his chest. His skin tightened. His mouth was dry. Something was very wrong. He couldn't see properly due to the water in his eyes, but his hearing was fine. His mother whispered prayers with mounting hysteria, while a different set of verses – deeper, more menacing – issued from his father's throat.

Albert had always been a bad boy. So it was destined.

Albert knew he'd always been bad. Even when he was trying to be good for his mother and father, he knew darkness worked within him. It was hard knowing everyone thought God had marked you when in your hearts, you knew it was the Devil. All his life he'd spread the word of God, looking to his parents to rid him of the demon in his soul. He had led sermons as a child; as a teenager, he'd warned others of the dangers of vice, smoking, sex and alcohol. He had stood over rows of expressionless faces to speak of sin, repentance and absolution in a voice that wasn't his own. Grown men had wept at his eloquence, priests had grabbed their wooden crosses and screamed in worship as he'd led them in frantic prayer.

He had protested outside sexual health clinics and the funerals of sinners; on more than one occasion he'd been present at interventions. He had always been a constant, soothing presence who helped calm those who knew him and his cause. He was their inspiration wherever he went with his parents. He saw their faith strengthen when he appeared at the protests, he felt their yearning to be close to him, hear him, touch him. But in the whispering night, he couldn't deny the truth: it wasn't him. The person who spoke of hellfire and damnation, who was going to lead the holy war for his people, was, despite his words and actions, wicked and depraved.

He continued battling to erase sin from people's souls and hearts, but none of it felt real. It was a show he was putting on. It was the words that people wanted to hear, the hope they were looking for, and Albert never wanted to disappoint. He stood before people and let the words come forth. Not for him, never for him, always for his parents. And God. Only when he was alone did he wonder which god did he really serve.

Albert had always been a bad boy. The truth would soon be clear.
They'd stopped throwing the water over him, but the sense of disorientation hadn't vanished. The prayers hadn't stopped either. He shivered; goosebumps started to rise, his skin tightened further and his teeth chattered. His t-shirt stuck to him and his soaking underwear clung to his genitals which were desperately trying to shrink back inside him. His mother continued praying. His father clutched the front of his t-shirt; Albert barely registered the pain as he grabbed a handful of skin through the shirt, ripping out a few of the thin hairs that had only recently grown on Albert's chest.

Behind the meaty fist that flew towards him, Albert saw the utter disgust on his dad's face. Then the punch caught him on the side of the head.

From down a hazy tunnel of darkness, he heard wails, prayers, and sobs. He knew the verses his mother was repeating, and the words spewing from his father's lips. He let them wash over him, and the darkness swallowed him again.

Albert had always been a bad boy. But he would serve another. The snakes coiled around his wrists brought him back to the world. The rough rope bit into his cold skin, ripping and chafing the flesh as it wound tighter with his every panic-filled movement. With his eyes tightly shut, because he didn't want to see, he tried to move forward and found he was tied to a chair. More ropes were wound around his legs, down to his ankles; had been knotted so tightly across his chest that he could only take the shallowest of breaths.

Albert fought to get his breathing under control and felt the panic lessening its grip. Slowly he opened his eyes, and his surroundings began to take shape.

He was in the kitchen. Sickly yellow walls, grease-stained and peeling, black and white linoleum jaundiced from years of nicotine and stained with years' worth of spilt food and blood. His mother stood by the oak kitchen table, a cigarette smouldering in the overflowing ashtray beside her. Purple-grey smoke snaked up and wound around his mother's face, tainting the air with its familiar stench. The years had not been kind to Maggie Harries. She'd been a beauty before her marriage at the age of eighteen to her one true love, with a joyous laugh and eye-catching figure. Before the hate within her had been awoken;

before she found Jesus; before she became the mother of a bad boy. Her once-slender legs and slender frame had thickened into near shapelessness, and her once-golden hair hung limp and streaked with grey around her doughy face. But her eyes remained bright; in fact, they burned. And they were locked now on her son's face, searching for something. She was looking for the devil in him, Albert knew. This wasn't his first time on the kitchen chair.

"Albert, you've been a bad boy," said his father, behind him. His voice always made Albert think of gravel being walked on by angry soldiers. Hard, demanding, and never far from anger; that was the voice of Albert's childhood. His mother's wavering whisper had never stood a chance at lodging in his head as had that of his father – the father above and below.

"You got something to tell me, son?" There was no missing the anger in his father's voice.

"No, sir." Fear and confusion made Albert sound weaker than he'd intended.

"Liar," said his mother. She took a deep drag of her cigarette, breathing fresh smoke into the air, and pointed at him. "It's the devil inside you speaking."

Albert tried to study her, to gauge the severity of what was coming. In his seventeen years, this was the only family he had known. Despite frequent prayers, to any god that would listen, for another.

"Ma...I don't know what you mean...I.." he couldn't find the words. The fear had managed to break free of its confines in his mind.

"You've been keeping secrets, Albert," his father said. Secrets were not permitted in the Harries household. "The Devil works through secrets. What is the fifth commandment?"

"Honour thy mother and father," Albert said immediately.

"And are you?"

The question hung in the air. A cold finger of fear moved inside Albert. He tried to move his arms but only succeeded in tightening the ropes securing him to the chair. Terror rendered him helpless. His feet were shaking; his heart pounding; his mouth was dry, and his tongue felt as though it had swollen till it filled his mouth. This wasn't like the other times his family had tried to expel the sin from him.

A memory of an afternoon sorting through family photos with his dad last year. The chance for the two of them to spend time together was always rare. However, Maggie's birthday was coming up and Albert thought a photo collage would be a nice touch to hang in the local church hall. They had sat reminiscing over a variety of pictures. Captured moments of love in their lives together. Shared memories and jokes bonding them more than blood. When his dad told him that he was proud of the young man Albert was becoming he could have cried.

"*Are you?*" his father screamed, ripping him from the warmth of the past. "*Are you fucking honouring us?*" Albert flinched. His father never cursed. "*Answer me, you filthy. Fucking. Faggot!*" *Albert had always been a bad boy. The truth was about to come out.*

His father strode out of the kitchen. His disgust felt like heat on Albert's back.

Albert's mother dragged her chair around the table and set it in front of her son. With a faint groan, she lowered herself onto it. It creaked beneath her weight. She lit another cigarette and looked at Albert. She reached forward and tenderly brushed wet hair off his forehead.

"How long have you called me your Mum?"

"Seventeen years." Albert could see the pain in her eyes. "Since you found me." What should he say next? "Since I was saved by you Mum."

"Exactly. You were given to us by God. We prayed, Albert. We prayed for years. For God to give us a child, to *bless* us with a child. And He answered us. He delivered unto us a son. You." She drew on her cigarette. "He touched you, Albert. You have the mark." Her eyes settled on the left side of his face. "His mark is on you, Albert. And you don't always live up to the responsibility that having it entails."

It always came back to the mark. His parents claimed Albert had been marked by God at birth and given to the only people who could raise such a child. He'd always known how he'd been abandoned on their doorstep without even a note, barely a month old. To hear the full story, he'd had to wait for a rare night of drunken honesty from Maggie. Disturbed from her prayers by a frantic knocking on the door, she'd found him wrapped in a blood-soaked towel. When she saw the cross burned into his face, she knew God had chosen her to save him.

They had taken him in and raised him. With scripture and verse, they'd shaped him. In smothering love and choking fear, they paraded him around churches to vomit out the hatred and disgust that the people there wanted to hear. But they were the only family he had.

It hadn't always been beatings for Jesus. There were happy memories amid the pain and self-doubt. He couldn't count the day's he'd spent baking in the very kitchen they sat in now. Maggie and her boy baking cake for the church raffle. Maggie Harries scones were always a talking point and a source of jealousy amongst the other wives. The memory of being pulled close to her as the sun warmed them both was amongst some of the happiest of his life. The safety he could feel simply by her side. The kitchen table where his dad had helped him learn multiplication. A rare trip to the cinema to see a cartoon he couldn't remember. There had been love in the Harries household. It might have been in occasional short supply. Yet when it bloomed, it washed away the stench of fear and pain. The Harries had shaped the young man he was now. The good and the bad.

"I'm sorry Mum." He felt a tear run down his face. "I'm really sorry for letting you down." His voice choked and he could feel more tears threatening, but he couldn't break eye contact with his mother. If she only saw how afraid he was, even Maggie Harries would respond. There was no trace of the woman who used to laugh as she passed him a spoon to lick clean. The mother who tenderly wiped clean his face when there was chocolate on it. The mum who had told him he was her secret blessing. There was only the woman in front of him now. There were no maternal feelings on her granite face. Just the rage. The rage for Jesus.

"Oh, Albert. You know how your father gets." If his mother saw his fear and distress, she chose to ignore it. She sighed and drew again on her cigarette. "He just gets worked up. He never means any harm." Albert looked down; he knew what she was about to say; "He does it for your own good."

As his heart broke, he felt the ropes around his wrists and legs tighten further. Holding him in place. Binding him to the inevitable.

"You need to get out."

The Voice was so clear this time that he thought at first that his mother had spoken, but she just stared wordlessly at him. He'd been hearing the Voice a lot lately, but always when he was alone; this was the first time it had ever spoken to him in front of someone else. It had been a soothing relief from his heartbroken prayers to a God, who according to everyone he knew, would damn him to Hell.

This was the first time he'd ever heard anything other than power in it.

"What's Dad going to do?" A stupid question, he already knew the answer. It would be a beating. *A beating for Jesus,* as his father liked to say.

"He's going to get the truth from you. He's worried about your soul, Albert. You're not like other boys. There's sin in you, and your father needs to get it out." The beatings for Jesus had been as much a part of his life as the bible. After a few years, they had stopped holding fear and were just another part of the tapestry of his childhood.

She rose from the chair and came towards him. "What's been going on with you and Rich?"

Time slowed and stopped; a slow, deep chill crept through him. His mother lit another cigarette; fresh smoke enveloped her and billowed towards Albert. Tobacco and fear filled the small kitchen. The scent of his childhood. He coughed.

An innocent-sounding question, but everything depended on what he said next. Like his father, his mother could smell a lie.

"Has the Devil got your tongue?" Maggie Harries moved closer still. "What sinful things have you and Rich been up to?"

The panic was rising in Albert's stomach, tightening his chest; a wave of goosebumps swept over his skin. She studied him with disgust and contempt.

His father should be back with his belt by now. This wasn't going to be a normal night of getting beaten for Jesus. Maggie Harries had caught the serpent in her house. The stinking lie that had been evading her for years.

The ropes felt so tight he was struggling to breathe now. Albert tried to speak. How had they found out? "Mum. *Mum*. I…we…"

The slap echoed from the kitchen walls. His face was almost numb from the water, but it felt as though his mother had hit him with an iron glove. She had never hit him before. That was his father's domain. She was the haven after the beatings as a child. Albert was beyond panic. He had never seen the ice-cold hate in his mother's eyes before.

"You kissed him!" She looked, and sounded, almost hysterical with rage. When he opened his mouth to speak, Maggie Harries leant forward and put her cigarette out on his face.

Albert tried to scream but could not. He thrashed in the chair in blind panic, but the more he struggled the tighter the ropes bit into him, holding the sinner in his place of penance.

"I am coming for you," said the Voice. *"Be brave, child."*

"Dad's back." His mother sat back down at the table and lit another cigarette. From behind Albert came the slow crush-shuffle of his father's feet. Judge, Jury and Father stepped into the kitchen.

"You've sinned, Albert." *Crush-shuffle.* "You went against God's teachings". *Crush-shuffle.* "You and that boy *Rich*." His father spat the name out with loathing.

Albert tried desperately to turn, to make eye contact with his father and tell him that he hadn't changed, hadn't sinned. but no matter how he twisted in the chair, Albert couldn't see him, and without looking him in the eye, none of it would matter. He just needed to tell him that he loved 'that boy Rich', that he wanted his family to love him back, that he wasn't a bad boy. He couldn't be brave. He needed his Dad. He needed his Mum. He needed them to hold him, to tell him he wasn't a bad boy, that he wouldn't burn forever.

But his mother wouldn't look at him. Her eyes were fixed in awe on the man behind him, and no amount of thrashing or turning in the chair brought Albert any closer to seeing his father. He only saw the man's shadow. It was time to face his sins. The court was in session.

"Dad...."

"Hush," his father ordered. Albert's plea died in his throat. "You weren't to blame, Albert. Sin is all around you."

"Amen," his mother sang.

"It's every person you meet outside this house. It's the radio, the television. It's the world we live in, Albert."

"Speak the truth." His mother swayed from side to side.

"But you were different, Albert. God marked you for brilliance. He put the mark of his first son on you."

"He is with you!" His mother's eyes began to roll in her head; her swaying gathered momentum.

"The mark has led sin to you. To tempt you. To make you fall from grace."

"*The Devil can't have you!*" His mother panted for breath, rocking faster and faster back and forth. Albert had never known fear like this.

"But God knew that son. He knew that you would be targeted. That's why he sent you protectors, to look over you."

"Amen!" his mother sang, quivering. She was with the Lord. The Spirit was working through her. Albert had seen this a thousand times in the past. He'd never been certain that it was actually the Lord working through his mother. Part of him thought it was an excuse for her to close her eyes and heart when a beating for Jesus was taking place.

"Dad, please," Albert begged, "Let me see you." Knowing it was futile, but unable to stop, he tried desperately to turn. The ropes had cut his skin; he could feel patches of blood begun spreading across his t-shirt. Still, he struggled to turn and face his Judge.

"God gave you to us," his father went on. "He named us your protectors. Your angels, to keep you safe from sin. Your family alone can help you fight this demon inside you." His deep voice had taken on a rhythmic tone, as though he were preaching to a crowd of hundreds instead of his terrified son.

"Amen," his mother added. She had stopped swaying and now stood upright and alert.

"It's our job to watch you. To drive evil away before you, and to look for it where you cannot see it."

"Amen." His mother's affirmations seemed to encourage his father. His shadow fell over Albert. The darkness was all he could feel. No matter how he craned his neck couldn't see his father, his mentor, his protector, his jailer.

"Dad." Please. Don't." But this wasn't his father; these were not his parents. Not the people who'd taught him to tie his shoelaces, read his Bible, bake bread and lead a sermon. Not the people who loved him. Yet these were exactly his parents. The people who taught him that God's word erased any violent action. That being different was a sin. They were the parents who he knew he could never confide in because his heart wasn't what God would condone. They were the parents who would, through their love, cut and beat the sin from their son. With a hymn in their hearts and a smile for Jesus on their faces.

"I am close," said the Voice. *"Be strong."*

"The Devil has presented himself to this family, Albert." His father's gravel voice stated this as fact. "The Devil was the shape of a friend. Someone this family trusted." There was no emotion in his voice. Only the righteous truth of the Lord.

"Dad, Rich isn't the Devil. He isn't. He said he.." *Loves me,* he wanted to say. But even in his darkest moments, there were words best left unsaid.

Memories of a stolen kiss on the walk back from choir. Of nervous glances and knowing smiles shared between them. Of a connection beyond that of parents and church. The dreams of a family away from Maggie Harries' watchful eyes.

"He wormed his way into this family; he sat and laughed as we prayed together. The whole time, plotting your downfall. Scheming on how best to hand you to the Devil!"

"No, he never," Albert whispered. He had no fight in him. Despite the Voice's urgings, he had no bravery left. He was alone. He was tired. His deepest fears had been given their moment and he was lost in them. How could he reason with the rage and hatred coming from his parents when they viewed it as love and concern. He couldn't cut through their devotion to an old God who believed in an eye for an eye.

"You were tested, son. You were given a chance to fight temptation and you failed."

"Dad, Rich isn't the Devil."

"He was a sinner!"

"Amen!" His mother screamed. Her eyes rolled in her head as she fell to the floor, screaming for Jesus. The table shook, and a cigarette fell on the linoleum beside it, still smouldering. Maggie Harries was in the throes of the Lord.

"Call to me, child. Call my name! Only I can save you!"

The Voice was screaming in his head. He could taste the force in it, the strength of certainty. He had never felt such strength before. Fresh waves of refreshed vigour started rushing through his body.

"Rich was the Devil, Albert. There's only one way to deal with the Devil, son."

"Expel him from your heart!" his mother screamed, as she hauled herself to her feet. She stared past Albert to the shadow behind him and moved towards it. The burn on Albert's face started to throb as if readying itself for another.

"We are your parents, Albert." There was no love in his father's stone voice. "Our job is to protect you. To guide you through the sins of the world and shield you from them."

"What have you done?" He didn't want to know. He already knew. Deep down, he knew that they did what *their* Jesus wanted them to do with all sinners.

"It is my job, as your father, to do the tasks that nobody else would. For Jesus, and for you." This was the man he knew. The man willing to do the tasks nobody else would do to and for his son. This is the man who once beat a man for throwing a cup of water over Albert at a protest they attended. He was also the same man who beat Albert so badly for singing along with a top ten hit on the radio that he couldn't get out of bed for three days. He was both protector and punisher.

As his father spoke, something heavy, wet, and unpleasantly warm landed in Albert's lap. Before he could look down, he met his mother's hard grey eyes. She was openly sobbing. For him, or Jesus? He hoped it was him.

"Don't look, child," cried the Voice. *"Call my name!"*
He knew the name she wanted him to call. A name was whispered by Rich during a whispered conversation over other gods. A name he said would protect and nurture them. A loving mother in the cosmos to counter the hateful father on earth. A deity Rich had taken to offering prayers to. How could a benevolent God allow their suffering to continue? He had posed this question to Albert during a walk through the fields one sunny day after church. He had offered up a list of alternatives. A list of names his mother and father would have cut their tongues out for uttering. One goddess had won the heart of the boy he loved.

His eyes were closed. He didn't want to see. But he had to. The scene had to be played to its end. He silently kissed the boy with the sun streaming through his hair and a laugh dancing on his lips. He had to know the source of the wetness in his lap. His fear was paralysing and energising. He knew who the voice belonged to. He knew how this would play out.

"Give yourself to me! Call my name!" The Voice screamed. It screamed in a thousand voices, voices that sounded like warnings, blessings, prayers. The warmth had run down his legs, pooling around his feet. It was sticky and wet. He closed his eyes tighter. His throat had contracted so tightly in his fear that he could hardly breathe.

"Look at the sin in your lap," his father ordered. Albert started to open his eyes.

"Give yourself to me, Albert. Call my name!"

He could taste the name on his lips. A name of power, once whispered on a pillow, by the gentle lips of the boy he loved. A name he'd almost forgotten, but now recalled clearly in his terror. He had to see. And so he did.

He saw his mother, gripped by hate; saw the smoke rising from the cigarette burn on the linoleum behind her. And then he saw the red.

There was so much of it. It covered the pink mass in his lap. It had formed a small puddle at his feet. It took a full minute to notice the pink mass' blonde curls because they were coated in red. Before recognition dawned, he saw the wet, gaping, holes on either side of what was once a nose. The swollen mouth hung open; the teeth inside were jagged and smashed. Torn red strings hung from the stump of a neck. The only person who had never thought of him as a bad boy had been punished for his hope. Here in his lap lay the price of his betrayal.

"I cut the sin from him," Albert's father said with unmistakable pride. "For you."

Albert screamed. He screamed in anguish. He screamed in fear. He screamed for release.

"Now, I have to remove sin from you."

The shadow moved. His father was circling him, the bloodied axe in hand. It had been sharpened Albert noted calmly. "Maggie, remove his underwear. I'm gonna have to cut you, son. Cut the temptation from you."

Something snapped. Darkness filled him. The name was on his tongue. The name that was screaming to be summoned. The name that would bring justice.

Martin Harries stood before Albert. Blood dripped from the axe and his short beard. Albert felt the head's weight on his lap, the tepid stickiness of blood coating his groin and legs. His mother's voice had risen as she prayed, almost to a shriek, and his fear and anguish gave way, at last, to rage.

"*Cailleach!*" he screamed.

Ten seconds later, they were screaming too.

CHAPTER ONE

The problem with having the best sleep you can remember is when your body decides to wake, you struggle desperately to hold onto the dreams you've been having. He could smell her perfume, feel her heavy breasts against him, her warmth against his naked chest. Her breath was an arousing caress against his neck as she nuzzled close to him, but in addition to her sensuality, she made him feel safe. Sighing, still half-asleep, he moved his arm to touch the woman who was awakening every inch of his body, the feminine shape that meant he was home, safe and loved, but he only touched the air. She was gone. Moaning, he touched the bed, but the sheets were cold and empty. Slowly, he opened his eyes and stared. It took him almost half a minute to realise that he didn't recognise the room.

He sat up, confused at first, then began to feel the first stirrings of panic. He was in a large, dim room. The off-white walls, with their old, cracked paint peeling from patchy grey undersides, were dirty and in desperate need of some kind of affection. There were no windows; the only light was a dirty yellow hue and came from a bare bulb hanging from the ceiling, coated in spiderwebs and dust.

The dark wooden floor was covered in leaves, broken glass, wrappers, and a thin layer of dirt. Footprints – years old by the

29

look of them – had been trodden into the grime on the boards. Piles of what looked like junk were scattered to one side. He jumped out of the bed, only to find he was naked.

"What the fuck?" he said aloud. He began to shake; goosebumps crawled over his round belly and through the body hair that covered him. Panic had hold of him now: he could feel his heart beating, hard and fast, and covered his genitals with his hands as he tried to take stock of his surroundings. There was a pile of broken bricks and what looked like a smashed chair in one corner, with some kind of blue material folded on top, but he paid it no attention at first until he'd turned a full circle and his eyes lit on it again. Covering himself with something would be better than standing here naked. He couldn't handle feeling both confused and vulnerable at the same time.

Gingerly picking his way across the cold floor, he let out a sigh of relief when he saw the blue material was a wrinkled blue t-shirt on top of the broken bricks. He picked it up and put it on; underneath it was shoes and a dirty pair of trousers. As he hastily dressed, he could feel something heavy in the back trouser pocket. The clothes were a good fit, and now he was dressed he felt less vulnerable. More able to face his surroundings.

How had he got here? He couldn't remember. It was worse than that: he couldn't remember anything. A short, muffled cry of panic escaped him.

Who are you? his mind whispered. *You might die here,* another, quieter, part of him added.

With all his willpower, he calmed himself.

"Start with your name," he whispered. He closed his eyes and tried to recall. He swallowed hard.

"Hi, my name is..." He extended his arm in a mock handshake, hoping that might jog some memory. Only silence greeted him. He covered his face with his hands.

He couldn't remember who he was. He didn't know where he was. In short, he was lost. He took three deep breaths, then slowly lowered his hands, and took stock of his surroundings once again, looking for any clue to who or where he was.

The air was stale with an unpleasant undertone that he couldn't place. The room was abandoned and without furniture, aside from a bare, filthy mattress atop a metal bed frame. He spied, with disgust, a grey, moth-bitten sheet in a pile at the bottom of the bed. The warmth he'd felt there now seemed tainted by the sight of the reality. There were no windows, no light switches or plug sockets, in the room, but there were two doors: one in the bare wall to his right, the other in the wall to his left.

"Well," he sighed aloud, "you've established you don't know where the fuck you are."

His chest was tight with fear. He wanted to shout for help, but knew, somehow, that it would be futile. Wherever he was, he was certain that he was alone.

Forcing himself to move, he crossed to the right-hand door, feeling the weight in his back pocket once again. He reached in and found a wallet. It was aged black leather and looked well-loved, with frayed edges and creases that showed its age. There was no money inside no personal photos, but there were a few plastic bank cards. The same name appeared on all of them: *Grant Wilkinson*. He felt something click. He knew the name.

"Grant. Grant Wilkinson." His voice was a croak, but he was relieved. It made him feel a little safer. He didn't know how or why he knew it, but this was his wallet. Which meant these must be his clothes.

The thin t-shirt was plain blue, with a dark stain on the front. His first thought was that it was blood, but he pushed the notion as far away as he could. He was having a bad enough day already. This was a problem for another time. The sleeves clung around his biceps; the shirt was tight across the chest.

The trousers were a nondescript pair of jeans. There was dry mud on the bottom and another dark stain around the crotch and knees. No underwear, no socks; he looked at the shoes. The bloodied white trainers were also a perfect fit. No doubt about it: that these were his clothes. He chose not to ask why he'd woken naked, why his clothes were scattered at the base of the bed and likewise refused to even think about the blood on his clothes. He didn't know and, at this moment, didn't want to. Grant Wilkinson had more than enough to work out for the time being.

"Okay, Grant. You know who you are. Now you have to figure out *where*." He looked at the two doors. Both were identical: dark mahogany wood, with elaborate silver round handles. They were the only things in the room that looked as though they'd been cared for. Fine dust hung in the air and covered everything in the room, but the doors were spotless. the wood was rich in colour, and even in the dull light from the ceiling, the silver handles shone. Continuing his original path, he crossed to the right-hand door. Rubble and glass crunched underfoot.

The door was plain enough in design. Aside from the craftsmanship on the handle and its cleanliness, there was nothing to make it stand out, still less to help him identify his location. He couldn't help shake the thought that this door didn't belong in such an unloved room. He crossed to the other door and inspected it: it was identical in every way. He shook his head, hoping to loosen a memory or a plan of action, then walked back to the bed, flopped down and put his head between his dirty palms, overwhelmed.

Hot tears burned his eyes, trickling down his face to stain the floor below. He hadn't intended to give way to his emotions, but it wasn't every day you woke naked in a strange room.

You don't know that for certain though, do you Grant? For all you know, you've lived in this room your whole life. He shook his head. He couldn't explain but he knew that wasn't true. The certainty that he'd been beyond this room brought him strength. Wiping his eyes, he stood up. "You're not going to get anywhere crying," he told himself.

He decided to try the doors. They'd probably be locked, but he had to check. He returned to the right-hand door, reached out and took hold of the metal handle.

He released it instantly, with a gasp: the handle was white-hot. A red mark was already forming on his dirty palm. Another second, and he would have had a serious burn. He put his other hand on the door itself and was shocked by the heat coming through the wood. It felt like the door to Hell.

He decided to try his luck with the second door. Having learned from the first handle, he only tapped his finger on the second one's raised edge. It was unnaturally cold. Confused, he put his hand against the wood. A wave of bitter cold passed through him; he shivered and pulled back.

A choice needed to be made. He could either try his luck on the Hell Door or open the other, to what must be an ice palace. "Let's see what's behind door number 2," he said aloud, without understanding the reference.

As if in answer, there was a quiet pop. Spinning around, he stopped halfway through a turn; the right-hand door had disappeared. Where it had been, there was now only a dirty wall. "What the *fuck*?"

He rushed to where the Hell Door had stood. The wall was the same as the others – chipped paint and dirt – and cool to the touch.

He felt that he knew very little, but he was confident that doors didn't just disappear. For now, he pushed the question aside, to join the one about the blood on his clothes. He turned towards the remaining door. He knew that he had to get out of this room; there might be answers on the other side of the wall.

In eight steps he had crossed the room. He didn't pause as he turned the handle; didn't allow his eyes to focus on what lay ahead as he walked through the door towards what he hoped were answers. In two more steps, he was over the threshold and free of the room, and the door slammed behind him. There was no going back.

BOOKS OF SARAH - BOOK ONE

I love this feeling. The first entry, in a brand-new diary. The excitement at getting to start a new book of my life. As usual, I start a diary and thank Mum – she gave me my first diary when I turned thirteen, told me that she'd written them all her life and it was a good way to see how much you've grown through each handwritten book. With the crack of the cover and a glance over the first blank page, I always feel like this is it – the start of a new me. I thought it when I was a teenager, and I can't see myself stopping any time soon. The timing couldn't be better either. Tomorrow is my wedding day! Talk about a new chapter of my life – just in time for a new book. The new me is going to be captured here, in these pages for the rest of my life.

I could be very girly here and just scream. I'm not like that sort of girl normally. I'm more of an average Scouse girl. Plain Jane really. I'm nothing special if I'm being honest, but that all changes tomorrow. Not only do I get a husband, but a new surname, too!

As excited as I am about being married, I don't know how I feel about giving up my name. Sarah Matthews has done me very well for the last eighteen years. I don't even know who Sarah Burns is going to be. Is she going to be a bitch? Or worse – is she going to be fat? Whatever happens, this is going to be my final entry as Sarah Matthews, Plain Jane.

I guess it's normal for a bride to have doubts before her wedding day. Mum even told me that the night before hers she nearly did a vanishing act! I couldn't believe it – my mother, Mrs "Do-As-You're-Told", almost did a runner on my dad! Dad just rolled his eyes – he'd heard this story a hundred times before. That's the thing about being together as long as they have, though: you run out of stories. I hope that doesn't happen to me – or at the very least, I hope Michael does a better job of pretending to listen. Mum's always been a talker, though – Dad's the quiet stoic one. Goes to work, comes home, has his tea and just generally grumbles until he goes to bed. Rinse and repeat (or he would if he had hair!) So he did surprise me when he said that I didn't have to do a vanishing act: "It's never too late to call this off, Sarah." I swear you could have knocked me over. He might not say much, my Dad, but when he does, you listen. It wasn't just that he'd chosen to whisper this after Mum had left the room; it was the look in his eyes. He looked so sad and – I'm sure – worried. I know he isn't Michael's biggest fan, but he must be able to see that I love him. They've got to; I never shut up about him. I feel it, though, when he comes round: the icy silence from Dad. The glances from Mum in his direction. The number of times they've asked us to stay in with them for a drink or a meal. Honestly! The way they're acting it's like I'll never see them again when I'm Mrs Sarah Burns.

I just wish they could see Michael the way I do. From the minute I met him, he's been the most important man in my life. (Sorry Dad!) I still remember him standing there in the club. I'd gone out with Sharon (slag) and Michelle (two-faced). We thought we were the best thing in the world. You do when you're sixteen, though, don't you? I was wearing my favourite LBD and Mum's heels. I've still got the dress, and I look just as good in it now! The Grafton was always busy on a Friday night, but Sharon "knew" the bouncer, so he let us in without checking our ID. At least her fanny was good for something.

After a few glasses of piss-like wine and a couple of smokes we'd bought together, we were ready to dance. Michelle was giggling like a hyena and Sharon had set her eyes on some scrawny guy on the other side of the club, but I just wanted to have a dance. That's all I ever wanted to do on these nights out, but Sharon and Michelle were normally out for blood. They approached a club, and boys, like a military operation. I just wanted to have a couple of drinks, dance till my feet hurt and get a kebab on the way home. At most, maybe a snog – I mean, everyone likes a snog on a Friday. Before I knew it, Sharon had decided to go and get her man. She pushed and shoved her way through the crowd like a wrestler making his way to the ring. She's the tank in our operation: she's a size 22 and has the biggest perm I've ever seen, so I couldn't imagine anyone standing a chance against her if she decided they were in her way. I didn't know Michelle was two-faced back then, so we started dancing. I didn't know the song, but it didn't matter. I just let go and let my body move with the beat. That's when I felt him looking.

Michael Burns. It was as though time slowed down the first time, I saw him. He was tall – at least six foot five inches of pure heaven – towering over his two mates. He was slim, but you could see he was strong by the pull on his t-shirt. Just tight enough to let you know that he had some muscle under there, the arms bulging slightly round the sleeves. Slicked-back brown hair and a strong face, with just enough stubble that I wasn't sure whether he'd come from work or if it was intentional. I couldn't stop looking, taking in every beautiful part of him. The music almost disappeared (soppy, I know!) when I looked into his eyes, and when he winked at me across the dance floor, I *literally* went weak at the knees. He had a cigarette hanging cockily from his lip, and he was smiling. Naturally, I blushed – I could feel my face going bright red after being caught looking at him. I tried to play it cool, but my eyes kept returning to him. And he caught me every time. That smile got bigger and more cock-sure with every look. Where's General Sharon when you need her, eh?

I managed to hold off for two whole songs. Two of the longest songs in the history of music. I wasn't even dancing at this point, more swaying in a loved-up haze and giggling like a schoolgirl. Sharon had come back upset; Operation Friday had ended in failure. "He's got a fucking girlfriend," she squawked, face quivering. "Fuck him. Not even arsed," she added, in a tone that told Michelle and me that she was in fact, very arsed. She continued her attack on the man, who she'd never know, with Michelle agreeing and nodding like a trained puppet. A slow song with a crap beat came on, so I told the girls I was going to the bar. That's where he got me. A single soldier, separated from the team behind enemy lines. I was obviously easy prey.

"Your mate's a dickhead," he said, walking up to me, that smile and those eyes trapping me. Up close he smelled amazing: beer, aftershave and masculinity, all rolled into one. My body was buzzing. "You don't even know her," I countered, trying to sound angry, but I was smiling.

"Am I wrong?" he replied. His deep voice and cocky attitude caught me off guard (or at least that was how I played it.) I turned, laughing, trying to get served. Pushing beside me, he put his empty pint glass on the counter and the bartender came over straight away. He ordered and turned to me.

"She's a dickhead," I agreed, and burst out laughing. He introduced himself and passed me a glass of wine. It was red wine and warm; I only really like white wine, but I didn't question it and smiled my thanks. How was he to know what I drank?

The rest of the night passed like a dream. Well, aside from Sharon battering the skinny guy's girlfriend and Michelle throwing up on herself. I didn't care, because I got to kiss Michael Burns. It was a deep slow kiss behind the taxi rank, and it was amazing.

I knew he was desperate to sleep with me from the first night, but he was so good when I told him that I couldn't do it unless I was married. I wasn't just about to slag it about, even if I was desperate to sleep with *him*. God knows I was. I could feel the hardness that throbbed against me every time he pulled me into a kiss. But I wanted to do everything properly. Most lads would have run a mile if their girlfriend asked them to wait, that she was a virgin and just wanted to give herself to one man. That's just who Sarah Matthews is. (Or should that be *was*? I don't know where the line gets drawn, this close to the wedding.)

It was a pretty slow courtship, really. He was twenty-three and had his own place, even a car! The girls were green! I felt like a princess whenever he was around me. Sure, his car was a bit of a banger and he usually made me put in the petrol but considering how much he drove me round it was only fair. He always paid, though. His place was a nice little two-bed terraced house. It was in dire need of a deep clean: you could tell a single man lived there. But it didn't matter – I've made little touches here and there. Always mopped through and hoovered for him. I even got him into the habit of letting me wash the bedding! Got to show you're wife material from the get-go, Sharon always said. She'd been with enough men to have a rough idea of what to do.

He worked on the docks, so he was always up early and in bed early. It meant that I only really saw him of a weekend, but every Saturday he'd pick me up in the car and we'd go for a drive and something to eat. I got to know him so well on those drives. The road seemed to disappear, and we'd tell each other all our secrets. I told him how I fought with my mum. He confessed to having nobody in his life. We connected on a level that felt old and true. He even proposed in the car. When I said yes, he cried a little. "You have no idea how it feels to have someone as my own," he said. I cried too. We kissed and caressed to celebrate the commitment we'd just made: the promise that for the rest of our lives we'd be together. We had just taken the first step on our journey. I don't think I stopped smiling for a week.

Dad wasn't impressed with the news. "You pregnant?" he asked when I told him. Barely even bothered looking up from his paper. I was furious. Mum just cried and said I was too young, that I was throwing my life away on a silly teenage crush. I told Dad I wasn't pregnant – if that's all he thought I was getting married for, he didn't know me at all! I told my mum to stop crying and that it was a lot more than a crush. That we were in love with each other, just like her and Dad had been. Michael apologised for not asking Dad for permission. Took him out for a drink and everything. He explained that he'd just been nervous, that he knew how much I looked up to Dad and that he was worried he'd never be able to live up to his legacy. Dad apparently looked him up and down before unhappily muttering his congratulations. Michael said it wasn't a great start, but every relationship has to begin somewhere. Mum spent at least two weeks ignoring him whenever he came to the house.

Dad just doesn't like Michael, and I don't know why. Mum finally came round to the idea, I suppose. I mean she helped me plan the day and even took me dress shopping. She did the whole Mum thing eventually, but every time she tried to speak to me about Michael she'd end up crying. You should have seen her absolute meltdown when I came out of the changing room in the dress I'd chosen. She ran to me and hugged me, telling me that no matter what she would always be there for me. I don't know quite what she was getting at but, but it was nice to just have my Mum back a little bit. I'd lost track of Sharon and fell out with Michelle so didn't have anyone to ask to be my maid of honour. A full-time, two-year relationship took a toll on my free time. Life just got in the way. Although some of the rumours that Michelle spread about Michael's ex-girlfriend are just too horrid

to repeat. The two-faced cow was just jealous that I could keep a man. Yet again, thank God for Mum! She's stepped up to the plate to act as both the mother of the bride *and* the maid of honour, all in one go. I just hope she can actually
 bring herself to smile on the day. The closer it's gotten the colder her and Dad have been about the whole thing. I overheard them arguing a few days ago about it. I should have felt bad, but I didn't. I'm a woman and can make my own decisions. Even if they think he's a "bad apple" (Dad's words not mine.)
It's only going to be a small ceremony. Michael has a few guys from work, but he doesn't have a lot of friends. Other than Mum and Dad, neither do I. There'll only be about eight of us in total. Not that it matters. After tomorrow it's me and Michael versus the world, and we'll see who Mrs Sarah Burns actually is!

27th March

It's official. I'm married. Mrs Sarah Burns. Goodbye Sarah Matthews. Goodbye you sad Plain Jane who never had anyone. Goodbye to the dutiful daughter and hello to the new wife. I can tell I've just turned a corner into the best experience of my life.

CHAPTER TWO

Grant hadn't meant to shut the door behind him, and the loud
bang made him turn at once to reopen it, but it was gone.
Vanished.

"Wha…?" He felt the smooth wall. Two vanishing doors in two
minutes? There was only so much he could push to the back of
his mind.

"Come on!!" he shouted. He channelled his fear and rage into his
foot, kicking the spot where the door should have been, but his
toes crunched against hard concrete. With a cry of agony, he tried
to grab his foot, lost his balance, and fell to the floor. He began to
sob. This was too much. He didn't know where he was, *who* he
was, what was happening to him. As he realised how little of any
of this he understood, he felt an overwhelming urge to give up.

"Giving in already?" a cold voice taunted. He didn't know if it
was his or not.

Curled up on the floor, without hope, he was close to doing
exactly that. He didn't know enough about himself to feel any
shame at the prospect. He didn't even know what he looked like.
How could you gather your strength if you couldn't even
visualise yourself being strong? He was a shell: an abandoned
mind in a strange body. Everyone had a self-image. Everyone

except Grant Wilkinson. The realisation brought a fresh wave of misery. He was lost and alone, with an unknown past and an uncertain future.

"What about Sarah?" the voice taunted. *"Don't you remember Sarah?"*

A memory came to him:

He can smell her perfume, feel a rare smile spread across her face as she pulled against him, her body's warmth. She kisses him: it's soft at first, tentative, then hungry. He runs his hands up her back and feels her tense as his fingers encounter ridged scars. Before she can pull away, he draws her closer and kisses her more deeply. She moans, softly. When they part, he looks, aroused, in love, into her brown eyes.

"I'll never hurt you," he whispers. Her expression becomes sorrowful, and he feels his heart breaking for her.

"I promise," he says, and kisses her again, aching to make her feel safe. "I love you, Sarah." Even with all the conviction in his voice, he can see that she is uncertain. He hides the small break in his heart with another light kiss.

The memory faded, but the emotions remained. He knew love. If he was lost, then so was she. Alone, he'd never survive here, but with her, with *her*, he could face anything. Fresh with purpose, caught up in the memory, Grant pushed himself to a sitting position, then halted to take stock of his location. He stood, wincing as he put weight on his injured foot, and slowly turned. The walls were off-white, the paint peeling from a patchy grey underside. A dirty wooden floor strewn with leaves, broken glass and discarded wrappers covered in a film of dirt. A bare, filthy mattress on a metal frame in the middle of the room; a single, dully glowing bulb hanging from the high ceiling, his only source of light in the windowless room. The walls had no plug sockets, no light switch, and there was a dark patch on the floor by the side of the bed in the same spot where he sat crying before. The stale air still tasted of something that didn't belong. He saw the filthy sheet on the bed and knew he shouldn't be there. He left this room to find answers. But here he stood again.

But this time there were no doors. There was no escape from this prison he had already left. Without thinking, he ran to the wall where the door should have been. It was unmarked. There had never been anything but a wall there. Just like the other room. *Sarah*, he tried to calm himself by remembering her name but couldn't because that led to the question *Where is Sarah?* and, after that, who *is Sarah?* The affection he'd felt was already fading, replaced by uncertainty. Glancing at his hands, he saw a gold wedding band on his finger. *Is she my wife?* He didn't know if it belonged there or not.

He took a deep breath, attempting to quell his rising sense of panic. He was close to tears again. Had he always been a crybaby? Crying when the stress became too much for him was growing to be a habit, and Grant was beginning to dislike it. *That's the thing with not knowing who you are. You get to discover all your flaws for the first time.* He didn't particularly like the cold voice in his head, but at least he knew it was his. Five deep breaths later, he slowly opened his eyes. The room was the same. Except that it wasn't. Not only had a door appeared on the south wall – one identical in every way to the one he'd used before, but the bed had changed as well.

Resisting the urge to run for the newly appeared door, Grant approached the bed. The single bed was now a double and the frame had changed from nondescript metal to ornate mahogany, with a thick headboard decorated with painstakingly handcrafted carvings and swirls. He didn't recognise any of the symbols etched into the wood. A few images reminded him of changing seasons, but he didn't fully understand why. He could almost make out the shape of a woman etched into the middle but whenever he tried to focus on it, she seemed to shimmer out of focus. The mattress looked fresh, almost new. There was no bedding on it. But there was blood on it, and worse: a mass of it in the centre of the large mattress, covering fully a quarter of the surface. He tried his best to pull his eyes away, but despite his best efforts he couldn't stop staring at what looked like portions of old greying meat. He saw a chunk of matted hair, at least two teeth and what looked like a decomposing brown hand.

Bright red, dark red and brown; heavy stains and light ones. Fresh blood that smelt of iron and old, dark blood that smelt of rot. There were pieces of what looked like ancient yellow bone, stained with stands of something in with the wet mass. He felt sick, tasted bile at the back of his throat, but just as he'd stopped himself from crying, he forced the vomit back down.

A dark object of some kind was sticking out the mess on the bed. His gaze kept returning to it, even though he knew he should just go through the door. That no good would come from touching the object on the bed.

But even so, he reached out – tentatively, to avoid touching anything else on the bed. His fingers touched the object. It was hard, cold, smooth, and solid. He felt his forehead grow damp, his heartbeat quicken, his mouth dry out. When he licked his lips, his tongue felt like sandpaper. He wrapped his fingers around the tip of what resembled a darkly polished stake. When he pulled at it, he was surprised at the weight. With a stomach-churning wet pop, the object came loose.

In his hand was a stone the size of a small kitchen knife but far heavier than its appearance suggested and coated with blood. Moving away from the bed he stared at the object. It was almost five inches in width, with one end tapered to a sharp point. The implement was caked in dried blood, and pieces of other, more solid material adhered to three-quarters of its length. Whatever it was, it was a weapon of some kind. Now he felt a little safer: he was armed and could defend himself. Against what, he had no idea, but the mere knowledge that he was no longer completely helpless eased the panic that had been close to overcoming him. The stone looked sharp and lethal. Turning it slowly in his hand, marvelling again at its weight, he used his free hand to touch the point, then snatched it back with a hiss. A drop of blood welled from his finger.

Grant nodded to himself and turned back towards the door. Whatever Hell he'd found himself in, he felt better able to face it now. He'd found clothing. He had a weapon. He could remember Sarah. Crossing to the door with new purpose, he took the door handle without hesitation Whoever Sarah was, he was coming to find her. But as the handle turned, a deep rumble sounded behind Grant, and the floor shook.

He released the handle and turned to see the wretched mess on the bed begin to move. As he watched, it gathered itself together, solidifying into something new, which began expanding as he watch. The fresh blood rolled back across the mattress to the thing that lay at its centre. With a speed that appalled him, the heap of moist flesh and rotten hair solidified. The bed began to shake; the ornate headboard groaned and bulged and cracked and thick black blood oozed out, flowing across the mattress to add substance to the thing on it. A maddening whine began to emanate from the centre of the mess. Quiet and light at first, but rapidly increasing in volume and lower in sound. It felt like the noise was reaching for his brain.

Grant wasn't sure how long he stood there staring at the thing; he couldn't comprehend what he was seeing, or even completely believe it. He was almost curious, rather than afraid, at the prospect of what it would become. The spell only broke when a mouth opened in the incomplete semi-solid shape that now covered more than half the bed and let out a howl. Grant screamed in revulsion, with a force he hadn't known he was capable of and fumbled for the door handle. The door opened into the uncertainty of a new room, and he fell through with a thud. He was still screaming when he pushed the door closed behind him, shutting the howling thing out. He stumbled back, lost his footing and collapsed to the floor. He barely noticed. He shut his eyes, but he could still see it. Terrified to open them, he used the darkness to pray to any God that might exist to make the thing disappear. His heart was trying to break through his chest. The fast rhythmic sound made it hard to hear his own frantic prayers. But his prayers went unanswered and unheard, and when the door flew back open, they stopped. Grant cried out again as a puddle of blood slithered into the room; he managed to get to his feet and ran at the door, slamming it shut on the skinless horror beyond. He was stood in the blood but kept his weight against the door as something wet and heavy banged against it from the other side. The door rattled in its frame and more blood seeped over the threshold. He put his back against the door and dug his heels into the floorboards.

A brief pause. Grant remained rigid. A gurgling roar made the door vibrate. *Brace yourself. Brace yourself. Brace yourself.* Something smashed into the door, so violently that it was forced ajar. His feet, slippery from the blood on the floor, slid out from under him and he landed with a jarring thud. Sharp pain exploded in his rear. He could feel the warm blood seeping through his dirty jeans.

Disgusted, Grant scrambled away across the floor, not daring to look behind him at what might be coming through the open door. He made it back onto his feet and turned, arm raised for battle. Against his better judgement, his eyes followed his bloody trail back to the wall.

The door was gone. There was only a dark stain on the dry wooden floor where it had been; the blood had disappeared along with the door itself. Grant felt suddenly sick, and before he could control himself, he'd begun to vomit. He fell to his knee and retched; his nose burned from acidic bile, his eyes streaming and sputum dripping from his mouth. His newfound strength had deserted him completely.

Gingerly he stood up at last and steadied himself. He felt faint and could still detect the stench of the creature, which triggered a fresh wave of nausea. He wiped his mouth with the back of his hand, realising only then that it was bloody. Hardly a surprise; he was having that kind of day. Or that kind of night. He had no idea what time it was. He rubbed his mouth against his shoulder in an attempt to clean it. He could taste blood. He wiped his hands on his jeans and pulled his t-shirt free of his stomach: the warm blood had soaked through to his skin. Leaning against the wall, he sank to the floor, shivering in shock and revulsion. He felt dizzy and weak; he was about to faint again.

Don't you dare.

Suddenly Grant felt determined to an extent he hadn't thought himself capable of. "Stand up," he said aloud. His body didn't respond. "Grant. Stand. The. Fuck. Up." Leaning back against the wall, he pushed himself back to his feet.

Without any shock, he saw that he was in the same room. As a trick, it was growing stale. The same walls, the same floor – but where the bed had been there was only an empty space: the room held nothing but rubble, dirt and leaves. He spied the stone stake amid the debris; dazed as he was, he hadn't even realised he'd lost it. He went and picked it up. It felt heavier than before or, perhaps he'd grown weaker. The weapon gave him no sense of security now. The creature he'd seen didn't look as though it could be felled by a sharp stone. Whatever it was he'd fled from, it would forever haunt his dreams. And it was still out there.

When he straightened up, he saw another door had appeared in the wall. Or rather, the door he'd previously travelled through had returned. Again, he felt unimpressed. He was learning the rules of the game, although he doubted he'd make it to the end. swaying with fatigue as he already was, he suspected he'd almost welcomed the inevitable. Until –

"Help me!"

The scream came from behind the door. The voice was young, female– but, more than anything, it meant he wasn't alone here, and that gave him new speed and energy as he ran across the room.

"Help!" The voice screamed again, shrill with terror. Grant threw the door open with one hand, raised the stake with the other, and ran into the fourth room.

BOOK OF SARAH - BOOK TWO

28th March

The new chapter of my life has begun. Now that the champagne has gone flat and I've got a ring on my finger, I don't know how I feel about being Mrs Burns.

Don't get me wrong: yesterday was amazing. I couldn't sleep the night before – I guess the nerves got me (as if the giant diary entry wasn't enough proof!) Somehow, though, I woke up so excited that I didn't even feel tired. I could feel the adrenaline coursing through me while my hair was being styled and make-up put on. My white dress was gorgeous, and Mum cried again when I put it on. It was simple but beautiful, fitted at the waist and knee-length. Thin silk, and white to match my shoes and veil. When I floated down the stairs, Dad looked at me with so much love that I could feel it. He almost looked sad, but I guessed he just knew that his little girl was going on a new adventure.

The ceremony floated by in a dreamy haze and as soon as I said those two little words, I felt complete. I knew I adored Michael, but once that ring went on my finger, I felt an even deeper well of love open in me. There were twelve people in all (Michael's friends brought dates and Mrs Dougherty from next door ended up tagging along) at the ceremony, but from the applause when we kissed for the first time, it could have been a thousand. I thought I was going to burst I was so in love at that point.

Money had been a little tight during the planning, so instead of a big fancy reception, Dad had asked his local pub if they could lay on a few sandwiches and put us all up. Since Dad's been drinking there for the better part of twenty years, they said yes. I hadn't expected them to hang banners and put up balloons; it really can be the little things sometimes. Michael kept me close the whole time. I was so happy about that – I just wanted to be next to him for eternity. Mum fussed over me and all Michael's friends kept giving him knowing winks and laughing. Dad just looked sad. I kept meaning to go over to him, but every time I tried to go Michael would grab hold of my hand, pull me close and kiss me, whispering confessions of love and compliments on my beauty. There would be other days to speak to Dad, to let him know I still loved him and that things weren't going to change too much.

I kept track of my drinking. I knew what was going to happen that night, and, despite my nerves, didn't want to be drunk. My first time wasn't going to be some drunken memory fuelled by cheap white wine. This was my first time, I wanted to make sure and enjoy the act I had put off until I was married. Unlike Slaggy Sharon who just gave it away to everyone, I was going to cement my love and tie my body to one man. Michael, on the other hand, was knocking pints back. I suppose it affects men differently.

After his seventh pint, his eyes bloodshot and his breath heavy with alcohol, he pulled me closer.

"I want to fuck you so bad, Mrs Burns," I swear, I've never blushed so hard in my life. "I'm fucking dying to feel your wet pussy."

The world stopped when he said that. Those filthy words. I looked at him; the disapproval must have been clear on my face. I didn't know what to say. I tried to pull away. I wanted to go to the bathroom. Clear my head. It was just the beer, but hearing him speak like that made me feel dirty. His grip on my wrist tightened, "Michael, I'm going to the bathroom," I whispered, trying to smile. I didn't want anyone to know what had just happened. I looked at him, but I didn't see the gentle man I loved. "My cock is fucking *solid*. I'm going to pound the fucking life out of you when we get out of here." As this filth was pouring out his mouth, he took my hand and forced it onto a large hard lump in his trousers. With the smile still fixed on my face, I let him. Mum and Dad were deep in a conversation and Michael's few friends were busy playing pool or chatting up the few females in the pub. I watched one of them chatting nervously to the barmaid's chest while another was gingerly touching the shoulder of a blonde woman at the end of the bar. They were just boys pretending to be men. Between the smell of testosterone and cigarettes, I started to feel a bit sick to my stomach.

"Touch it," he whispered bringing me back to the here and now. With a firm grip, he began forcing my hand into a circular motion, then let out a breathy sigh and rolled his eyes. "Mrs Burns...." he whispered in a voice dripping in desire and need, before letting go of my hand. I yanked my hand back instantly, looking at him and for the first time seeing a side of him that I can honestly say I hadn't even known existed until then. A side I didn't like at all.

I excused myself and left him smirking at the booth. Mum gave me a questioning look as I rushed past, but Dad said something that caught her attention so they went back to the conversation they'd been having. I made it into the bathroom a second before the tears started

"It's the booze," I told myself. "He's just drunk and being stupid." But if that was the case, why did I suddenly feel so dirty? So absolutely terrified of what would happen when we left the pub and were alone in his – no, our – house? I took some deep breaths and tried to get myself under control. Mrs Sarah Burns wasn't going to be a crier. She was going to be a strong woman. I dabbed my eyes with cheap toilet paper and stared at myself in the mirror. My mascara hadn't run; my eyes were a little red but people would chalk it up to tiredness from the long day. I was a woman now. I would go out there and face my husband, and I would give myself to him tonight. I was acting like a silly school girl. Of course, he wanted me to touch it – he'd been patient enough to wait until today, and as Mum always says, men think with a different brain to women.

Feeling more in control, I left the bathroom and went back to my husband, picking up a large glass of wine on the way. The rest of the afternoon passed in a haze. I dulled my nerves with cheap glasses of wine, drinking until my head buzzed and time took on a thick, bouncy quality. Before I knew it, we were being ushered out of the pub by Michael's friends. The night was full of their jeering laughter, as they congratulated Michael on what he was about to do. He seemed to lap it up, full of winks and subtle comments, he even smacked my arse hard enough that the sound filled the night air. This was greeted by a laddish cheer that made Mum and Dad wince. I stumbled into the taxi, tipsy and reluctant. Michael slammed the door and coldly watched me correct myself. I could have wept; this wasn't how the day was supposed to go.

Our journey to our new home lasted fifteen minutes that felt like years. The silence between spoke volumes. The driver tried to initiate small talk, but after a few minutes, he realised it was futile. Michael looked at me like a piece of meat, smirking like the cat that had got the cream. With a deep sigh, he leaned back in the taxi so the bulge of his erection was plain to see. I tried my best to be excited by the prospect. I silently tried to chide myself for being stupid and acting like a nervous virgin. Although the truth was simple – I *was* a nervous virgin. "Can't believe you belong to me now," he whispered. His hand snaked into my lap, stroking the curve of my leg. At that moment instead of feeling aroused, I felt disgusted by his touch. I couldn't forget the ugly side of him I'd seen in the pub. After too short a time the taxi stopped outside my new home. Michael opened the door and got out, but due to the springs in the door it bounced back and I had to put my hands out to stop it from hitting me. Michael didn't even notice as he leaned through the window to pay the driver.

With a heavy hand on the small of my back, he guided me through the front door. I stood in the hallway, stupefied. I'd been here countless times over the past two years and had always felt at home, but today I felt like a stranger, uncertain how to proceed. My mouth was dry, my heart racing. I'd bought a silk nightdress for tonight – it would be the last time I could truly wear white – and when I'd tried it on the feel of the material against my skin had been almost erotic. I know that's not a very ladylike thing to say, but it's true. I'd been as excited about tonight as Michael, or at least excited about the idea of it. It wasn't every day that you lost your virginity. I wanted the act to be a joining of our hearts, a union to cement our love for one another. It clearly meant much less to him. I took a deep breath, reminded myself it was probably the drink and the banter from his mates. Maybe now we were home I could relax a little and get back to my pre-wedding day idea of how tonight would go. I reminded myself that I'd made Michael wait for this, so of course, he was eager. I just needed to relax.

He came up behind me, his beery breath warm on the nape of my neck, and grabbed my breast, hard; I let out a shocked gasp because I was in a world of my own. He pulled me into his body and rubbed his hardness against my rear. He moaned quietly, trying to tweak my nipple. "I can't wait to make you moan," he sighed, the other hand pulling my skirt up. I tried to pull away, "I should change," I tried to giggle and act naive, hoping to postpone the inevitable. "Fuck changing," he snorted, his fingers now trying to pull the side of my knickers down. "No, Michael," I said, panic rising. *It was not supposed to go like this.* I tried to pull away, but his arm became a steel rod across my chest, holding me against his cock, which poked into me to remind me of my new duty. "I'm going to make you scream," he muttered, as he finally hooked a finger into my knickers and roughly yanked them down. They only made it a third of the way down my thigh but it was enough for his fingers to try and start exploring. I struggled, pitting my rising fear and horror at the situation I was trapped in against his alcohol-fuelled strength. The struggle between his and my designs on the night felt like it lasted an eternity, instead, he suddenly let me go; I fell forward and landed on the floor. All I could feel were my knickers halfway down my leg.

Embarrassed and afraid, I stayed there, tears in my eyes. "Go on then," he said, pulling a cigarette from a battered box, "Fucking change." With that, he turned and weaved his way down the hallway.

I stayed there, on the filthy carpet, (he hadn't even thought to hoover yesterday) my head spinning, trying not to cry. Where was the gentle man I had fallen in love with? Who was this hard, uncaring monster that had pushed himself on me? I got to my feet, determined to be strong. I was married. The time for being a young girl was over. I rationalised that it was the beer and the excitement of the day, possibly tiredness. I was drained, and there was so much pressure on him it was surely only natural that he might lash out a little. Besides, he had waited. He hadn't complained or raised an objection when I'd told him, early on in our courtship that I intended to wait until our wedding night to give myself to him. It might be misplaced excitement. As Sharon told me, years ago, sex is different for men. With these thoughts racing through my mind, trying to calm myself and silence the confusion, I followed him to the kitchen.

Michael's house wasn't big. It only had two bedrooms, a small sitting room and a mid-sized kitchen with space for a table and two chairs, where he now sat. An open beer sat untouched before him. Cigarette smoke snaked around him, and the smell of grease was thick in the air. He turned slightly as I entered the kitchen,

"Thought you were changing," he said, his tone icy cold. "Sorry," I said meekly, unaware why I was apologising but trying desperately to fill the silent gulf that seemed to have developed. "I just wanted..."

Even now I don't know what I wanted. Before I could finish, he jumped to his feet, sending the beer flying across the table, strode the short distance between us and grabbed me by the shoulders. "Wanted what?" he shouted, shaking me. My head snapped back and forth. "To fucking prick tease me again? To fucking wind me up with your pussy and then not let me have it? Is that what you fucking wanted?" Spittle flew from his tight lips.

I didn't have a chance to respond; he pulled me forward and kissed me, forcing his tongue down my throat, the taste of cigarettes and beer turning my stomach. I tried to pull away, but he was stronger. His hands moved from my shoulders to my rear, cupping my buttocks and pulling me against him. Against his hard cock. I tried to pull away, putting my hands on his chest to push him back. He opened his eyes, his mouth wet, and smirked, "Oh, she wants to play the virgin does she?" His hands were now working his belt, undoing the buckle. "Michael, you're scaring me," I whispered before the tears betrayed me and began to fall. I swear he grew in size at hearing that.

He seemed to fill the room, our size difference apparent to me for the first time. "Scared? Awww. The 'ickle virgin is scared of the cock," he sneered, pulling the belt free. I was too afraid to speak. "Don't worry 'ickle virgin. Daddy's going to take care of you." He wrapped the belt around his knuckles. "Daddy's going to show you, there's nothing to be scared of." With his free hand, he cupped his crotch. "If you look after Daddy, you've nothing to be afraid of." Releasing his crotch he stared at me. "But if you struggle... well, Daddy will have to punish you."

I wanted to scream, I wanted to turn and run out the door into the night. Back to when he was my sweetheart and I was his princess. I wanted to go back twenty-four hours to when he was a kind and caring man. To the day before that when I wasn't owned. I wished I could back to being Sarah Matthews with her naïve view on love and the romantic dreams of a wedding night. "Now," he said, ripping me back to the life of Sarah Burns. "Get on your knees."

I had a choice to make at that moment. I could fight him. I could stand firm, slap him and walk out. Sarah Matthews wouldn't allow herself to be treated like that. Unfortunately, she had died this morning. Sarah Burns didn't have any fight. It had been scared out of her. The only fight Sarah Burns had was to make sure that her marriage lasted more than a night.

I lowered myself down. My knees clicked and rested uncomfortably on the cold tiles. "Good girl" he muttered. I looked up to him, his face looming over me as he undid his trousers. With a sigh, he let himself out. I've never been more afraid of anything in my life. It was bigger than I had ever imagined it could be, thicker than my wrist and an angry purple head. It glistened in the dull light, slick with his juices. "Suck it," he ordered, his eyes never leaving me. I put my hand on the base, trying to steady its throbbing jerks. At my touch, he moaned and got harder. I could feel it pulsating. "Put it. In. Your. Mouth," he hissed. Fresh tears fell as I opened my mouth and put the tip in. Salt and disgust filled my mouth as he pushed down my throat; suffocating, I tried to pull myself away. In response, he put his hands on the back of my head and pushed further in. Gagging, suffocating at the solid threat forcing itself down my throat, I could feel my stomach heave. All my attention focused on trying to breathe, trying to get away from him and to air, I could hear him murmuring encouragement and moaning as he slowly thrust, ignoring my struggles. I could hold it no longer; vomit pushed up my throat, and I retched. He jumped back, prick glistening as I turned to the side and threw up over the tiles and my dress, sobbing and gasping for air. He was laughing. Suddenly I was angry. Sarah Matthews was making a surprise appearance and spun towards him. "You bastard..." I screamed, before his belt-covered fist connected with my jaw.

I went down, landing in the puddle of vomit. Its warmth seeped through my beautiful dress. My makeup was smudged and smeared across my face. The side of my face was burning, but before I could comprehend what had happened he was on me. I screamed as he yanked me to my feet, ripping the bun out of my hair. I grabbed his wrist, trying to take the pressure off my head. He threw me across the room. I landed with a thud against the cupboard. With two giant steps, he was there. His cock was hard again, and he pushed himself back down my throat without a word. In my shock, I couldn't fight him. He pushed further down. I welcomed the lack of breath. I felt a light-headed sensation as he pushed back and forward, his moans the only sound I could hear. I could feel the darkness closing in. I could have laughed – the virgin died being choked on a cock. Oh, Sharon would have laughed.

He withdrew, and air flooded my lungs. Against my wishes, my body took deep ragged breaths. I returned to my body. A vessel I no longer wished to inhabit.

"You beautiful cunt," he said lovingly. I even believe he meant it. He looked at me with such love in his eyes that, for a split second, I saw the man Sarah Matthews had said yes to. With that, he shoved a kitchen towel in my mouth and pushed me to the floor.

I had heard the term 'foreplay' before, from my friends. I didn't realise that to Michael Burns, 'foreplay' was me suffocating and vomiting. As my head banged on the tile, stars appearing in my vision, he thrust his hand up my skirt. From his dry probing fingers, I knew what was to come. I didn't fight. As he entered me I cried. His largeness was painful and warm. I could feel the stinging as he pushed deeper. I was detached. Sarah Burns got raped on the kitchen floor, her silent tears ignored as her husband consummated their marriage with a rage and anger she'd never guessed existed in him. "Mine. You. Are. Mine," he whispered, in a rhythm matching his thrust. "You." *Thrust.* "Are." *Withdraw.* "Mine." *Deeper thrust.* Sarah Burns stared at a stain on the ceiling as he spilt his seed in her. She welcomed the emptiness as he withdrew. He stood over her, his cock still hard, wet and dripping. She lay there as he laughed and lit a cigarette. Vomit covered the empty shell of a woman that she was. Sarah Burns had seen a snapshot of her life.

It's official. Mrs Sarah Burns has made a terrible mistake.

30th March

I don't know if I can do this.

CHAPTER THREE

He was in a large room. The walls were off-white, the paint peeling away to show a patchy grey underside. No windows. A dirty wooden floor was strewn with rubbish and debris. Leaves, broken glass and wrappers, covered in a layer of dirt. A single bulb hanging from the ceiling, its harsh yellow light casting shadows around the room. No switches or plugs on the smooth, decaying walls. It was the same room he'd already traversed. The only constant he seemed to know now. But true to the nightmare he found himself trapped in, the constant was broken.

Broken by a girl screaming on the bed. The same bed he'd woken up on hours before.

"Help! Please help me!"

She could only have been thirteen, at most. Golden blonde hair shimmered in the harsh light. Her green eyes pleaded with him, full of terror.

"Heeeeeelp! Please!"

He was frozen.

It wasn't the girl who had caused him to stall, hands by his sides, slack-jawed, not even breathing. It was the thing attacking her. Writhing at the foot of the bed was a red bloody mass in an almost humanoid shape that defied logic and comprehension. It smelt of blood and wet rot, and it was shrieking as it pawed at the girl. He couldn't see the front of the creature, but the sound escaping it jarred his brain and made his testicles shrink. The wrongness of the noise was felt by every cell of his body. It was a mix of a pig's cry and a child laughing. It sounded like grief and pain. The joy of a child's birthday and the heartache of a funeral. Love and hate. Nails on a chalkboard; the soft touch of an old lover. Chunks of thick matter fell away from the creature as it flailed to get hold of the screaming child, landing with wet slaps on the floor, where they continued to writhe and added to the chorus of noise. Grant watched in further horror as the mewling pieces of wet flesh tried to crawl back to the creature before melting into blackened puddles of liquid on the floor.

"Please, mister!" she screamed. "Please! It's going to kill me." The hopelessness in her voice, the sheer defencelessness of the girl, spurred Grant to action. With a roar of his own, before he even knew he was doing it, he charged.

His shoulder connected with the beast's back. He had expected a solid mass but encountered spongy wetness instead. He had also hoped to throw the thing off-balance and gain the upper hand in some way. Instead, it twisted its gore covered head round and let out a wet roar. The girl seeing her chance started to move up the bed. The bed frame shook in her frantic journey drawing the creature's attention back to its original prey. In an instant, it lunged forward and what constituted its hand grabbed onto her leg. She screamed in utter horror and a wet sucking noise rose from their contact. As the same maddening, contraindicative noises escaped it, Grant grabbed at the monster's shoulders. "Get off her!"

His fingers sunk into the loose mess. Black and red spongy flesh squelched as he fought to get a solid grip. The creature shrieked, as if in pain at his touch. The girl was screaming now in wordless terror, and scurrying up the bed away from the beast, which now turned to face its assailant.

While the monstrosity had a human-like shape, the resemblance ended there. Its face, if it could be called that, had two deep holes where its eyes should be, sunk deep in which were yellow teeth, which protruded at every conceivable angle. The hole at the front that served it for a mouth yawned and stretched to emit that maddening shriek. Thin, needle-like fangs circled the circular 'mouth', and as the beast stretched open its maw, he counted at least six more rows inside what must be a throat. "Run," he shouted to the girl. The beast turned in the direction of his voice and let out another shriek.

He fixed his eyes on the monster in return. The weight in his hand seemed to call to him. The creature was pointed at him, a deep clicking emanating from somewhere inside it.

This beast's very existence unsettled him, it was so fundamentally *wrong* that it filled Grant with a dark rage.

Tightening his grip on the stone stake, he realised he wasn't afraid at all. As he stared at the creature he could almost feel it working its way into his mind, unlocking every dark thought and desire he had ever felt. The sensation was liberating in its maddening honesty: he wanted to kill this beast, to rage and beat it with his hands. Feel its bloody wetness wash over him as he undid whatever had created it. He would bathe in its blood, embracing the darkness that it had unlocked within him. Desire stirred in his crotch; murder awakened in his mind. Grant was so wrapped up in his dark desires that he never noticed as the morbid mass of the monster rippled from top to bottom. "Watch out!" the girl shrieked, but it was too late. A twisted bloody arm with new clawed fingers swooshed towards him, as he tried to step back on suddenly clumsy feet. Half stepping away, he escaped the brunt of the force, but not the claws, which slashed through the thin t-shirt and into his flesh. The creature had adapted itself to his new attacker. When it was just the girl he could feed without interruption or danger. Something the bloody chested Grant posed to it.

The acidic pain was instantaneous. Glancing down he saw blood oozing from the four thin lines that crossed his chest, and something snapped: the urge to inflict violence and pain flooded him as white-hot pain burned in his chest and heart. The girl was forgotten. He avoided another swipe from the claws of the beast and screamed at it, then laughed in mingled horror and hysteria. The stake was heavy in his hand. "C'mon," he taunted, circling the monstrosity. Had he ever been in a fight before? He couldn't answer with any sense of honesty, but his body reacted like that of a seasoned pro.

Grant faked to the right, then moved left, drawing the beast away from the bed, where the girl lay curled up into a rocking ball, sobbing and praying. All of which were irrelevant to what was happening around her. He would beat this creature, or he would die. The need to control something about this nightmare existence he found himself in clawed at his psyche.

The beast shambled towards him, long arms swinging and clawing for him. The pain in his chest intensified as more blood seeped out. With a confident feint to the right, he managed to circle the creature. It was big but slow. He used this to his advantage, lunging forward and using both hands to drive the stake into its back. The beast roared in pain and rage, and Grant gagged as a stench of faeces, rot and blood filled the room, It flailed helplessly, trying to pull the stone from its back. Grant charged once more, knocking the monster off balance. As it fell, he scanned the room and saw a large chunk of masonry at the foot of the bed.

Grimacing at the building pain in his chest, he ran and picked it up with both hands. The girl was white with terror, curled up and sobbing. "Don't watch!" he shouted with more force than he'd intended, and she shut her eyes as he shuffled back towards the heap on the wooden floor.

The creature was writhing in pain. The noise had changed: it was wailing now. Its slick wet flesh and limbs contorted as it fought without success to remove the stake. Something had been unlocked in Grant, the red mist that had descended with frightening ease was driving now. He was no longer fully in control of his actions – this was a kill-or-be-killed situation and his body was reacting with all the fight it had. The abomination made a weak attempt to swipe at him as he neared it, but he easily avoided its reach. He didn't hesitate as he raised the stone above what passed for its head. He started down as its maw worked and wailed; then, roaring, he brought the stone down in a smooth arc, connecting with the fragile flesh below. There was a wet pop as the "head" cracked underneath; rearing back up, he repeated the action until a flattened mess of gore atop a twitching heap was all that remained.

He let go of the stone. "Drop rock. Death," he chuckled, and collapsed, darkness swallowing him. He vaguely felt small hands shaking him as he lay there, and the burning slashes across his chest. "Drop rock," he chuckled again, amazed at his strength. "Death" he sighed; then his eyes closed and he drifted off.

#

*In the darkness, he can smell her feminine perfume, feel the
warmth of her heavy breasts against his bare chest. Not just any
woman. His woman. Her lips touch his in a kiss: soft, tentative
and hungry. He runs his hand up her back as he pulls her closer,
feeling her tense as he touches the ridges of scars, reminding
them both of a truth that they are desperately trying to avoid.
Before she can pull away, he kisses her deeper. A moan escapes
her. Aroused, in love, he looks into her brown eyes. "I'll never
hurt you," he whispers. "I promise." He kisses her again,
desperate to make her feel safe. "I love you, Sarah."
She allows herself to be held, the act of love still fresh for them
both, a heady scent of sweat and sex hanging in the air. "He'll
kill us," she whispers into his chest.
"Shhh." He tries to soothe her.
"You don't know him." The steel in her voice whenever she talks
about this always catches him off guard. "He's insane."
With this admission, the gates open. Her body shakes as she
begins to sob. He can feel his heart breaking; how can anyone
hurt the person they love? How could anyone hurt her? She
aches for love and protection. As she cries in his arms, he swears
he will cross the fires of Hell to protect her.
"We should run away," he suggests, holding her tighter, and
kisses the top of her head. "Just go. We don't even need to pack.
I've got a friend in Scotland who can put us up." He pauses,*

knowing the next sentence will carry power. "He'll never find you." Words tumble freely from his lips: plans and promises that he knows are meaningless even as he suggests them.

She stops crying and pulls away from him, holding the sheet over her naked body, trying to preserve her modesty. Her eyes are full of pain. "You'd do that?" she asks, quietly. "Just leave your life here? For me?"

"In a second," he responds and grips her hand. "You need to get away from him, Sarah."

She looks down. "It's not that simple."

He's about to speak, to tell her and explain just how simple it would be for them to fulfil the romantic notion of riding off into the sunset, but she holds up a hand and silences him. Two fingers are twisted, a permanent reminder of the time her hand was broken for burning a shirt with the iron. Or the subsequent refusal to allow her to go to the hospital, her fingers had never set properly after that. She rubs them constantly; the pain has never quite left. All of her scars carry a similar story, and their pain never quite leaves her. Silence hung between them. He can see she is readying herself to say something big. Something that would change them forever.

"It is. We get in my car. We go. He'll never know." He's whining, almost begging her to buy into the fantasy. He'll take her far from here, far from the city that houses her abuser, from the pain

and abuse that has dogged her life for ten years. Even now he
can't imagine surviving what she's endured in her ten years of
marriage that have been her prison. He has never wanted
anything more than to whisk her away from the hellish life she is
trapped in now. "I have money, Sarah. Savings. We could use
them."

Those sad eyes look back at him again, silencing his ramblings at
last.

"I'm pregnant" she whispers, and bursts into tears.

#

He awoke with a scream. Sitting bolt upright, he scrambled to his
feet, his body aching and burned. Unsurprisingly he was still in
the room. His off-white prison. He was alone; scanning the space,
he spied a door on the right-hand side. The girl must have fled.
There was a bloody mess a foot from where he had lain, and a
cloying smell of rot. He gagged but swallowed the bile back
down and studied the abomination.

A puddle of blackish blood had congealed around the corpse. The
smell of decay was so thick he could taste it; flies buzzed
hungrily around the shape. Even in its death, the aberrant thing
held power over him. What hell could this creature have crawled
from? He noticed, with a trace of panic, that the stake had been
removed from its back, leaving a gaping hole. The girl must have
taken it when she fled.

He touched his injured chest, grimacing as he pulled his top away from the wound. He felt fresh blood trickle out, but the pain was a reminder of his victory.

He was exhausted. Even the small sliver of hope that the child had represented had begun to wane. The creature was clearly diseased: he would not be surprised if he died of some kind of blood poisoning, and a small part of him would probably welcome it. There was nothing else to be achieved here; with a final glance at the mass on the floor, he crossed the room and opened the door.

Instead of walking through, he stood at the threshold for a second. With absolutely no surprise, he saw that behind the door was a replica of the room he stood in. With a sigh, he walked through, and the door clicked shut behind him.

He was back in the large room. The walls were still off-white and the paint continued to peel in various degrees from a patchy grey underside. There were still no windows, and the only source of light was the familiar single bulb. Leaves, broken glass and wrappers were still scattered across the dirty wooden floor and covered in a thin layer of dirt. It was the same room he'd already travelled, the same four walls that he was growing certain would be the last things he ever saw. The smooth doorless walls no longer concerned him. He knew how this would go. He just had to wait for a door to appear.

The only difference this time was the lack of a bed. In its place was a single wooden chair and table. With heavy limbs, he walked over to the chair and collapsed onto it with a sigh. Had he ever been this tired before? He didn't know; his only memories were of the horrors he was still enduring. The girl, whoever she was, felt like a dream, her screams a distant song he wasn't sure he'd even known the words to in the first place.

He glanced at the small side table beside the chair, his heavy eyes threatening sleep with each blink. He allowed himself a minute in the comfortable darkness. His breath was slow and deep. A light breeze caressed his face. Slowly, he opened his eyes and saw a glass of water had appeared on the table. His mouth ached for it. He hadn't eaten or drank since he'd woken and running on pure adrenaline had taken its toll on his battered body. He picked up the glass, wincing as the movement disturbed the fabric of his torn shirt, aggravating the cuts on his chest. Cautiously, he inspected the water. It was clear, and the glass was cold to the touch. He was parched, his throat tight with thirst. He licked his lips; his tongue felt like sandpaper. Was he really going to drink it? Considering how little he knew about his surroundings, the idea of drinking a glass of anything from here didn't seem like a good idea. It could be drugged or poisoncd, to kill him while he was weak or send him to sleep to continue the assault on him. He thought all of this, then downed the liquid in three gulps.

Ice cold shivers assaulted his stomach as the water hit and he felt his insides cramp as the water sloshed around him, but it was crisp, clean and satisfying and a semblance of strength began to flow through him. A simple glass of water restored something that he hadn't known he was missing. He licked his lips and put the glass back on the table with a clink, and now saw a small plate had appeared. On it was a sandwich. He laughed lightly. Whatever was going on, at least his host was kind enough to keep him fed and watered. He picked the plate up, already knowing he'd eat the contents but unable to resist checking.

Between the two slices of stale bread were pink layers of meat, an inch thick in all. Although it was dry and tasteless, he devoured it in four bites, and a hunger he hadn't known he felt abated. The glass was full once more, and he drank again, a burp escaping his throat as he stretched. He felt somewhat invigorated. He half expected the plate to refill with another sandwich, but when it remained empty, he wasn't surprised.

A door had appeared on the wall in front of him. It was time to continue his journey. He put the plate on the floor and brought his foot down hard. With a satisfying crack, it snapped into four pieces. Taking the largest piece, he ran his finger over the edge. It was sharp enough to use as a weapon. He ripped one of the torn parts of his shirt off and wrapped it around the base of the fragment. He might be continuing, but he was refreshed and had a weapon. He had seen horrors, but there was a young girl in here with him too, and the knowledge that he didn't have to continue alone gave him new strength. Was she Sarah? It didn't feel as though she was, but nothing was certain at this point. Either way, he intended to find out. Walking with a new purpose, he opened the door and went into the next room.

BOOK OF SARAH – BOOK THREE

23rd September

I lost my baby this week. My body rejected her. Not that I know it was a her... but I did. I could just tell. Mothers know these things. She was supposed to be my gift from the universe for surviving the last three years. The universe has a sick sense of humour.

Sometimes I can't believe it's only been three years. There are days that feel like they've lasted an eternity. The days when he comes home from work full of rage and anger and I'm all that he can take it out on. Then there are the times he brings me flowers and tells me that he didn't mean it, that he knows I should leave him and how lucky he is that I forgive him, his sobs and apologies filling the prison I call home. He says these things, forgetting that he locks me in the house, won't let me work or make friends. Won't let me go anywhere but the local shops without him on the rare days he unlocks the door. I think I prefer it when he beats me. At least I know where I stand then.

Michael was excited about the baby. He laughed and said it was a belated twenty-first birthday present. (Not that he *got* me a present.) I was so scared when the line turned blue on the pregnancy test. I'd had to sneak it into the house, terrified by the changes in my body. I knew deep down what the cause was, but when I saw the undeniable truth, I cried. It was the last thing I wanted. Why would I inflict this life on anyone else? I'm not naïve enough to believe that a baby would fix everything. But underneath it all, part of me was glad that I wouldn't be alone and would finally have someone to be better for, someone that might finally give me the strength to leave. I loved her from the second I saw the test.

When he came home that very night I showed him the test. I can honestly say I'd never seen him so happy. He was full of promises that this would change us. That his son would be this and that. He took me out for a meal to celebrate. It was the first time since our wedding day I'd felt special. His pride and happiness were contagious. Before I knew it I'd forgotten – briefly – how much I hate him, and for that short time, I was happy. I was proud. I was Sarah Matthews.

After Dad's death last year Mum and I had a big falling out. She's never forgiven me for not going to the funeral. I couldn't tell her the real reason I didn't go, she had enough going on without me telling her that Michael had beaten me so badly I couldn't stand up for a week. Oh, Michael went, even he knew that there was a semblance of keeping up appearances to do. He just told everyone I'd given myself food poisoning from my terrible cooking. She'd phoned me the next day and told me in great detail how I'd broken her heart. How both her and my dad had raised a spoiled child. She said Michael had been a rock to her, but told her all the horrible things I'd been saying about them both. Both of us were sobbing on the phone when I tried to explain that I wanted to be there more than anything. It was my last chance to say goodbye. Since the wedding, I had seen them less and less. Michael always seemed to feel uneasy under my dad's watchful eye. Dad noticed things, despite being a quiet man. I think back to how unhappy he was with me marrying so young and how angry I was with him. I think now I realise he might have just been unhappy with the man I'd chosen. The number of times I saw Mum put a hand over his to stop him from saying something when we did go round, should have been a sign.

After a few months of silence, Mum sent me a letter to say that she couldn't cope with the house anymore. There were too many memories of Dad everywhere and it was breaking her heart to live there without him. It was the most she'd ever spoken to me about her feelings, maybe the letter was a way to get it all out. Sort of how I use these diaries. She said that she was moving away to go live with my Aunt Sheila in London to get her head sorted and gave me Sheila's phone number and address. She apologised for the argument and said that Sheila would always have room for me. There was even money to cover a train ticket. I think now that she knew what was going on. This was her way of offering me an escape. I sat dazed reading the letter. If I went to London he'd never find me. I picked up the phone and called mum's house but it just rang out. I tried for a solid hour to get through but I never got through – Michael came home and my routine kicked in. I'd been stupid and not hid the letter or the money in my upset at not being able to speak to my mum. To the woman who really did love me and wanted me to get away to safety. Michael can barely read, but he took the money and put it in his wallet. He put the letter in his pocket and never mentioned it again. When I built up the courage to ask him about it three days later he said that he must have lost it. He also mentioned that he had changed the phone number to the house. His tone made it clear this was not something to discuss further. I cried that night, admittedly I cried a lot, but that night I cried because I knew I was finally alone. I only had Michael.

A baby changed things. I wasn't going to be alone anymore. I'd have something that loved me just as much as I loved it. Despite the rough road we had travelled, I felt the threads of a family getting woven together. Whether I want to admit it or not, that's what Michael and I are. A family. A unit. The baby would give us both something to dote on and it would help, I felt it in my bones. Michael had talked about how alone he felt growing up, how his parents never showed him affection and he promised he'd never let his son feel that way. I saw him then, the lost boy he must have been growing up. The man who I'd fallen in love with. Michael Burns was cruel and hard but underneath there was love. My life wasn't easy with him, I can see that. He's wicked at times and the pain he's caused me will never go away, but a baby changed all of that. He promised me that it would all change. He'd never touch me again and I believed him.

For three glorious months, we were Daddy, Mummy and Bump. He opened the door and let me go shopping as I saw fit. He bought me flowers and last night he actually cooked for me. (It was awful and everything was burned but he was trying.) We actually laughed as we both took a bit of the chicken he'd cooked to discover it was too dry to eat. We ended up eating chips from the chippie straight from the paper and that night he held me so close to him I forgot. I forgot the beatings. The cruelty and the pain. I forgot the way he treated Sarah Burns and for a few brief hours, I was Sarah Matthews again. I'm not ashamed to say, it was the best I'd felt in years. It's amazing the thirst for affection you can develop when it's not poured out. I drank that night. I was quenched. It was a ruse though. It was life-giving me a small cup of hope before knocking the glass out of my hands.

When I woke this morning, he was downstairs. I could hear him banging about and I was sure he was whistling. I stretched and felt something wet below me. The world slowed as I lifted the duvet. That's when I saw it. Blood. My body had decided to betray me. Haemorrhage my happiness into an old pair of dishwater white knickers. I screamed. I wailed. I distantly heard Michael running up the stairs. I couldn't take my eyes off the dark stain down my legs and under my body. I turned and looked at Michael, tears starting to fall down my face. For a split second, we locked eye's and I saw it. The undeniable fact was written plainly across his shocked face. I was alone again.

27th September

Normal service has resumed. A two-week reprieve to "get over it" and he's back to being the man I married. I'm firmly back to being Sarah Burns. I was waiting for it though. His face when the doctor told him I was unable to carry a baby full term. He knew then that it was my fault. That I wasn't strong enough to do my duty as his wife. You wouldn't believe how much I cried that night. How much I've cried every night since. I'm crying out every drop of affection and love I've drunk in the last three months. I don't deserve it.

It doesn't seem to matter as much anymore. I'm so full of pain at this point I barely feel the punches and kicks. When he forces himself inside me I don't struggle. I let him do whatever his sick mind can come up with. I watch it happening to me from time to time. I go completely still: I feel every bit of the pain in my heart,

I let that pain fill me completely. It's a bitter drink I swallow to replace the honeyed taste of happiness. I silently curse every God there was and will be for taking my baby from me. I cast my spirit out, and in between the desperate curses, I pray. I beg and plead to any entity that will listen; "deliver me from this life." Then I open my eyes and I'm standing next to myself, looking at the poor creatures in front of me. Him, so full of hate and rage at the world he has to torture another human to give his life a purpose. His once-beautiful body twisted on the fear he drinks daily. His once handsome face has started to darken from the rage he wears daily. Once where he could command a room through his laughter, now he lurks watching. Waiting for her to step out of line so he can exact his own form of punishment. The light of anything good in him has been replaced with the shadow of anger and hatred. Her, so weak and fearful she stays with a man she knows will kill her, so terrified of being alone that she'll endure everything he does to her and more. Her youth and vibrancy punished from her face. A nose set wrong, a near-permanent hunch as she spends her time scurrying around. She tried to exist as small as she can get her body, unaware of her pain screams in the infinite cosmos. I watch as he lies grunting on top of her, whispering obscenities, spitting at her and pulling her hair. I pity her. Surely he must know, from the vacant look in her eyes, that she's begging the cosmos for another life?

When he's done, I close my eyes, and I'm back in my body. It doesn't work every time, but it's a welcome relief when it does. He's all but stopped talking to me. He blames my weakness for losing his son. Nothing to do with the three years of beatings I've endured: I'm just too weak to carry his child. If I could feel anything, I'd be hurt. As it stands, between the two of us, we killed our baby. Him by reducing me to a weak shell, and me for staying for so long. What else can I do though? I have nowhere to go. Mum has gone to London and I don't know where she is. He saw to that. My friends are distant memories relegated to flashes of nights with the girls and silly jokes. Everyone has moved on. The world has kept turning while I languish in a prison I helped to build.

He fucks me every night, although his heart isn't really in it. Last night he just got on top of me, came inside me and went to sleep. It was refreshingly short. I just lay there as he snored, realising that I hadn't spoken to a single person, him included, in four days. Only to myself, but I always do that. For the three months of the pregnancy, he never locked the door – for safety I assumed – and it's still unlocked now. I could have gone out and spoken to anyone, but I didn't. Maybe this is why the caged bird sings – she doesn't realise that she's in a cage.

28th September

I went outside today and bought a pint of milk. After yesterday's realisation, I thought I should at least try and leave the house. Besides, Michael threw the milk bottle at me this morning, so we needed more. I built myself up to it while I was mopping the floor. The silence in the house was becoming too much: I needed to hear noise, to hear people, and to prove to myself that I could leave the house on my own.

I ignored the two closest shops. I was enjoying the walk, the fresh air, the people going around their business, the general buzz of life that's easy to forget when you lock yourself away. The best part was that everyone was too wrapped up in their own lives to even notice me drifting through them. I've begun to think that I'm a ghost. I've left the world and I'm tethered to Michael. As I slip past people talking and laughing I shrink into myself. Nobody looks at me.

I realised, though, that I still wasn't actually speaking to anyone. Without thinking, I popped into the next shop I saw, grabbed a bottle of milk and walked to the counter. I tried to force a conversation with the older woman as she scanned my purchase, but she could only stare at my black eye. The pity on her face was all-consuming. I practically fled from the store; the electronic beep of the door sounded as though it was mocking my defeat. In my panic, I didn't pay attention to where I was going and my mind ran away with itself. What if she phoned the police? What if they came for him? Why hadn't I ever gone to the police? Why was I still with him? Why was I still alive? When will he kill me? And the one that really haunts me: What if he doesn't?

I was no longer in control: everything I've tried to suppress about the past three years came flooding back. I refused to be a beaten woman crying in the streets, something for them to gossip with their friends or workmates about, another bruised woman crying about a man, but tears were threatening, I could feel them stinging my eyes. I refused to let them fall. I wouldn't let them see any weakness. If he didn't get to see me cry, then neither would anyone else.

I had to find a distraction though. I've had these bursts of mental strength before and they never last long. Coming out of my head, I realised two things. Firstly, nobody was looking at me. Secondly, and probably more importantly, I was lost.

I could already feel my strength draining (why are you so stupid?) The *whys?* were turning into *WHYS?* I looked at my watch I'd been walking for over an hour. (Why are you going back?) I had no idea where I was. It was a busy road, people were milling about, casting occasional glances at my black eye before looking back down at the ground. I was no longer a ghost. I had become something that caused people to look away. To avert their eyes where possible to stop seeing the pain plastered across my face. There were shops behind me, but I couldn't cope with any more pitying looks. Across the road, however, was a library, a small community one by the look of it. I decided to cross over and go in. I know it sounds stupid, but it was almost as if I was being drawn there. An invisible hand of fate pushed me across the road, soothing the screaming in my head.

The interior was, for lack of a better word, cosy. There were two people behind a desk area, a kind-looking older woman and a man a few years older than me. They smiled at me when I walked in and went back to their conversation. No lingering looks, no pity hidden by a sad smile; I was pleasantly invisible. I let go of a shaking breath as I melted back into the shadows. I could be a ghost again. I took my time walking through the rows on rows of books, occasionally touching them, content to be lost in happy silence and imaginary worlds.

I felt safe for the first time in a long time. I was visibly invisible. People sat around, lost in their paper adventures. Without thinking I walked to the woman behind the desk and asked for directions home – and about how to get a library card. I haven't stopped smiling since I left. Even now, as he's snoring upstairs in a beer-fuelled sleep, I'm smiling. I've got everything ready to go back tomorrow and sign up for that card.

If I'm going to lock myself away in here, I might as well try and read while I'm doing it. They say books are portable magic. I could use some magic in my life right now.

29th September

I got my library card today. It might not seem much to some people, but to me, it's a trophy. Proof, and a promise, that I won't let myself hide in the house seven days a week. I mentioned it to Michael last night, he scoffed and said he wasn't bothered if I wanted to read books as long as it didn't cost him anything. He suggested getting a cookery book or two. I was barely listening, just nodded and said that I would.

As I walked back to the library today, the crisp air and gentle breeze made me feel as though I was getting aired. It was as if I was saying goodbye to an old part of my life. Isn't that dramatic? Probably, but right at this second, I don't care. I can be dramatic if I want. I've got three books next to me and I managed to have a full twenty-minute conversation with Jean (the kind woman from yesterday) about what the library can offer. She showed me around the small building and never mentioned the bruise on my eye or asked me if I was all right. She just spoke to me like a real, genuine human being. I never realised how much I'd missed that. I was treated like an equal. I even made a joke. It was a silly joke, but she laughed. Jean helped me pick my three books (checked out for two weeks). I got a silly romance book that she suggested, a cookbook and a book about a family of witches in New Orleans. I figured I'd try all three and see which sticks.

I'll make sure that Michael doesn't ruin this, I'll learn to be the best cook he's ever met. I'll push my brain in ways it didn't know it could go and every two weeks I'll go and refresh my choices and speak to Jean. Maybe I'll even speak to the man who works there. He smiled at me on the way out, and I started blushing. Not the most mature reaction, but I know that not all men are like Michael. It would be nice to speak to one who doesn't make me flinch when he moves.

Chapter Four

The room was empty. He didn't know what he'd expected to find, but it hadn't been this. There was a single door, directly in front of him. Relief washed over him as he lowered his makeshift blade. He crossed the room quickly, nervousness lending him extra speed. He didn't dare look back as he tentatively opened the door. The next room, unsurprisingly, was a replica of the one he'd left. Standing in the doorway, not fully trusting the experience, he scanned the room. It was empty. No bed, no debris: a hollow empty room lit by the same single bulb as all the others. Experience had taught him that the doors weren't always visible at first, so with a deep breath, he walked in and allowed the door to close behind him with a loud click.

He waited nervously for a few minutes for a new door to appear. He was still uncertain about the rules of his surroundings, but when the light flickered and went out he barely managed to stifle the scream that jumped to his throat. When the light came back on, the door behind him had gone. He was trapped. Panic began to build inside him, but he'd done this dance before and just had to be patient. Slowly he paced around the room, waiting for a horror to be overcome, a door or death to appear. He knew that all three were a distinct possibility.

He wandered the room; with nothing to focus on, walking became a tedious exercise. He used the time to go over what little he remembered; on his second lap of the room, he reminded himself that his name was Grant. The third and fourth laps were spent on the question of Sarah and his dream. Had it been real, or some cruel trick his mind was playing? He had a ring on his finger, so she guessed her to be his wife. He wanted so desperately to believe that. It felt like a small bit of hope that maybe there was something at the end of all this. Whenever he thought of her, there was a sense of love and commitment.

By lap seven his thoughts had turned to the question of the girl, which continued to dog him through his eighth and ninth trips around the empty space. He spent the tenth and eleventh laps trying to unlock some memory of what had brought him here. He touched the wall as he walked past it. It was physical and very much there. Someone had to have taken him to wherever he was. Whatever prison he was in, surely it had a warden. No matter how much he searched his mind, he never got any answers, just some deep frustration at the lack of knowledge.

He knew the question he was dodging though, the one thing he had been determined to not think of finally pushed its way into the forefront of his thoughts – what that thing was he had fought. *"Killed, you mean"*. A cold voice whispered in his mind. He looked at his hands and saw the dried blood on them. *"It came quite easily to you didn't it?"* the cold voice mocked him further. Shaking his head to dislodge the voice, he shoved his hands in his pockets and carried on walking. The voice didn't stop whispering fully, it carried on a steady monologue about how he had failed everything in here, how he couldn't be a person if he didn't know who he was. He did his best to ignore the facts that it kept trying to bring into the light. These weren't the answers he was looking for and something about the cold edge to the voice didn't lend itself to being an honest account.

On his twelfth lap of the room, he heard a noise coming from behind the wall. Goosebumps prickled his arms, the skin on his balls contracted and the voice in his head fell silent. He stopped and turned to face the wall, tightening his shaky grip on the blade. It was a slow quiet scratching, the kind you would expect from a small animal, but after everything he'd seen here so far, he doubted a simple rodent would be the source. A memory of the creature from the previous room danced in his mind. Its inhuman hand scratching to let Grant know that it was still here. He shuddered and took a step towards the wall.

As abruptly as it had started, the noise stopped. Against his better judgement, he approached the wall and touched the aged plaster. The second his fingers made contact with it white-hot pain exploded in his head. Crying out, he fell to his knees, dropping his weapon and clutching his temples.

"You don't know him. He's insane," a female voice whispered to his right. "You don't know him. He's insane," a deep male voice boomed in his left ear. "You don't know him. He's insane," a child's voice laughed, at his feet. Voices surrounded him, repeating the same phrase. First one voice, then two, three: a hundred voices, a thousand, their tones overlapping. Laughing, crying, screaming, moaning all around him. All uttering the same phrase: "You don't know him. He's insane."

On his knees. Grant let out a scream. The voices surrounded him. Touching him, caressing him, scratching him, he felt an invisible hand stroke his crotch. "You don't know him. He's insane." the chorus continued to whisper. He could almost feel the human behind the gentle caress on his skin. Its warmth provided a strange comfort. "You don't know him. He's insane," an invisible presence screamed in his ear, as another unseen hand scratched his face so deeply an angry cut appeared below his eye. "You don't know him. He's insane," a child giggled; fingers dug into his side, trying to tickle him. The noise surrounded him, the voices drilling deep. And then the symphony of dissonance stopped, as abruptly as it had begun.

Slowly opening his eyes, he saw he was still alone. There was still no door. The only addition to the room was a white plastic clock on the wall. Cheap and without character, it looked as though it belonged in an office. It had no hands and only even numbers. Before he could consider it further, a voice whispered: "He'll never know." His stomach dropped. Those were his words. A memory started to rise in his mind. "He'll never know," another voice laughed coldly. "He'll never know," a woman giggled behind him. "He'll never know," a menacing male roared in front of him; he felt spittle on his face "He'll never know?" a soft female voice asked. "He'll never know!" replied a harsh male one. The chorus of his words pushed the memory out of his reach. He knew that he had said that. Just not where. Not when. But he knew it was to Sarah.

He could feel fingers working through his hair, caressing his hair. Another pulled sharply, yanking his head back in a painful tug, exposing his throat. He prayed that this might be the end of the nightmare. "He'll never know!" the soft female voice whispered as thin fingers wrapped around his neck, squeezing lightly. "You don't know him. He's insane!" a dark voice whispered as the fingers tightened. "He'll never know," a child laughed as an invisible foot kicked him in the back. He fell forward as the grip grew tighter still. Stars appeared in his vision. His instincts told him to fight back as he desperately fought to draw breath. "HE'LL NEVER KNOW!" a different, stronger female voice screamed as another pair of hands pulled his hair so hard it came out by the roots, throwing him back on the floor.

"You don't know him. He's insane," a female voice giggled. Grant began to thrash frantically, trying to prise the unseen hands from his throat. His strength was rapidly leaving him, the harsh light from the single bulb began to dim. He knew he was going under. At that moment, he wanted to. To let the darkness take him to the source of these screaming voices and let them do what they would with him. His limbs grew heavy. "He'll never know," a voice hissed. "You don't know him. He's insane." The strength left his arms and he let them fall, defeated. "He's insane?" someone suggested. "He's insane," a female replied. "Insane," a child laughed. "Insane," the room agreed. Grant closed his eyes and let the darkness take him.

With a gasp, he sat up, filling his lungs with air. He was on the floor, but still alive. His throat hurt, so he had to take shallow, rasping breaths. Grant looked round. He was still in the same room as before. Although he couldn't be certain. Every room had been identical. He realised that whether he moved room or not was immaterial, he was alive. Despite the willingness to let the darkness take him, he was still here. He wasn't sure if he was glad or not. The voices were gone, but who knew how long for? Shifting position, he realised his crotch was wet, and let out a groan. He'd pissed himself. Shakily, he got to his feet, body aching.

Numbers had appeared on the clock on the otherwise featureless wall. It was still missing its hands, but at least something had changed. Whatever the puzzle was in this room, he'd set the wheels to solving it in motion. He didn't know whether to laugh, cry or scream. The noise that escaped him was a combination of all three.

His legs were stiff and his back ached from his time on the floor. He had no idea how long he had been out for, but despite the wet patch on the front of his trousers he needed to relieve himself. Walking to the far right corner, he undid his zip and urinated. "You beautiful cunt," something whispered menacingly behind him. Dick in hand, he turned, to be greeted by emptiness. A fresh wave of terror washed over him. He finished and shakily zipped himself up. He could feel the cold irritation from the wet patch on his skin, and the stale smell of urine that he had missed before. He surveyed the room, eyes lingering on the handless clock. Fear clawed its way from the back of his mind to take its rightful place as his primary emotion but as with everything that had occurred since he'd opened his eyes, he'd have to wait it out and deal with the aftermath in the next room, if there even was one. And if he made it there. Pushing the fear down as far as he could, he settled down to wait.

Silence wrapped its arms around him as the time passed. At first, he tried to count the minutes, but that only made him drowsy. He did laps around the room, but when he reached one hundred and thirty he stopped. Then he began to speak to himself in an effort to dislodge his memory loss.

"What's your favourite song, Grant?" He didn't know. At this exact moment, he couldn't name a single one.

"Your first crush was..." He had no answer. He only knew one name other than his own.

"Your favourite colour is...." a blank in his memory.

All he could remember was this place, and her.

Sarah.

Just her name made his body ache. He didn't know who she was, but he needed to find her. To save her. From what, he had no idea, but he knew he needed to save her from something.

After what felt like days he stopped walking. His back hurt, his feet throbbed; the damp stain had dried, but the stale smell of ammonia hung around him, stinging his nose and reminding him that discomfort was his only companion for now.

Despite his loneliness, he welcomed the silence; he had no desire for the voices to return. But return they did. "You beautiful cunt," a gruff voice whispered in his ear. Before he even had a chance to be afraid, he was flung across the room, hitting the wall with a thump before landing in a heap on the floor.

"Drop rock. Death," an invisible child giggled beside him. Grant lay there, dazed and in pain. His arm throbbed where he had collided with the wall, and the terror was back. His head swimming, he felt fingers lightly caressing him. "Daddy's going to take care of you," the air growled, before spinning him around, pressing his face and stomach against the rough wooden floor. Grant felt a sudden weight on top of him; the air was pushed from his lungs, and the bulb began to dim. In the quasi-darkness, all he could hear was his rapid heartbeat, all he could feel was the pain in his arm, wrist and throat. He was nothing but pain but knew the ordeal was just beginning. He screamed in horror as he felt the hands moving lower.

Rough invisible hands began pulling at the waistband of his trousers. "Daddy's going to take care of you," the darkness whispered as his trousers were pulled down, exposing his rear. Pure terror washed over him. He would not let himself be used like this. The weight on top of him laughed as he tried to move his hands to frantically pull his trousers up. He felt his insides churn as the realisation of what was about to take place was cemented. A fresh, violent need for survival awoke in Grant. "Fuck off," he screamed to the empty room, but heavy probing hands forced his buttocks apart. "You beautiful cunt," a distinctly male voice whispered in his ear as he tried to push himself off the ground, to stop what was happening. He would fight this with everything he had. He buckled his body and tried to twist his hips to make the invasion more difficult. He snapped his teeth at thin air when he felt the invisible hands near him. "Stop," he sobbed, as he was roughly pushed back into his original position. The invisible hands went back to their work and his cheeks were once more forcibly parted despite his efforts to clench them. Grant let out a sob. "Please. Don't". On the floor, he could see dirt and dust. He could almost count the dust bunnies that had gathered in the corner. He tried to focus his mind on something. Something outside of what was taking place around him. The heaviness on his body moved and ground him further into the floor. His arms were forcibly pulled out to each side.   His tears were a mix of fear, frustration and horror at what was happening to him. The floor drank them hungrily.

"You deserve the world," his invisible assailant moaned and spat on his exposed anus. It was ice-cold, drawing a shaking gasp from Grant before he felt a finger push its way into him. It was cold, and he screamed. "NO. Stop. Please." He tried to buck, to fight, to protect himself against this violation. But his arms were pulled and the little breath he had was coming out in frantic gasps. "Please. I'll do whatever you want," he begged the empty room. "Anything but this. Please". A chorus of laughter erupted around him. The room might be empty, but he was not alone. The finger probed deeper, stretching and violating him. Concealed eyes watched him; hands without substance pinned him to the floor. With a violent jerk, the finger was removed,

"Daddy's going to take care of you," a different voice promised, one he almost recognised. "Michael?" he asked the empty room, then screamed in pain as something large and cold was rammed into him.

White-hot agony spread from his rear as a chorus of laughter erupted around him. Whatever had been shoved into him was getting bigger. "You beautiful cunt," a thousand voices sighed around him, and then the invading item was aggressively removed. A sudden wall of silence fell around him, and Grant lay, broken and abused, on the floor, sobbing helplessly. The floor continued to drink his tears greedily as he lay there. He was too afraid to move for fear of drawing the unseen threats attention again. Something had broken in him. He could feel the shards of the person he used to be breaking away from each other. Whether he survived this experience, for a hundred reasons he would not be the Grant from before. This however. This would never allow him to heal. This invasion had taken more than he had to give. It had taken the essence of himself. "You bastard" he sobbed to the empty room before breaking down and sobbing. He sobbed from a pain so deep in his soul that the tears began to pool on the floor. Even it couldn't drink tears this bitter.

After a while, he felt a small vestige of strength return to him. Shakily, he pulled his trousers up, wincing at the movement. He lay there, and a wave of nausea washed over him. The phantom invader had left him sore and too scared to examine any damage that had been done. Summoning his dwindling willpower, he got to his feet and leaned against the wall, breathing heavily. He could ignore the pain, but not the dirty feeling that was now crawling all over him.

He was, as before, alone. This time he was certain of that. There were no voices around him. A glance at the wall showed him that hands had appeared on the previously empty clock face. It was ten past one. Whether it was the morning or the afternoon he had no idea, but the very suggestion that time now existed for him helped to keep him from going mad. He watched the hand move down as time passed; part of him was convinced that the clock would break, a final cruel torment to push him over the edge. The moving hands were the distraction he needed. He focused as much of himself as he could on the slow progress of time.

He felt the air in the room shift. To his right, another door had appeared. Slowly he moved towards it, wincing with each step. Hands shaking, he reached for the handle, then let out moaned as it refused to turn. The room hadn't finished with him yet. Screaming, he kicked and punched the door; it didn't even shake. "Sweet dreams," a female voice whispered behind him. As if on command, he collapsed on the floor.

#

Time was running out and they both knew it. She looked down at him lovingly as blood soaked through his shirt. He could feel his heart slowing. Tears sprung to his eyes. "Sarah," he whispered, her name light and sweet on his lips. She was close to panic; her eyes were full of tears and looked frantically around the room. He didn't remember how he'd come to be here, lying on this floor with a knife in his chest. He couldn't move his arms and his vision was darkening. All he could see was her. "Grant..." she sobbed. "I love-"

But before she could finish, another voice boomed in the darkness: "YOU FUCKING WHORE." As he sank into the darkness, he heard her scream. He had found them.

#

Grant sat up with a shriek, feeling instinctively at his chest. There was no knife. Under the grubby blood-soaked shirt, there was no wound, not even a mark. Sitting upright on the floor, he glanced at the clock. It was seven-thirty.

Thus began his wait.

After the first hour, Grant realised that the slow passing of time was worse when you could see it happening. His eyes never left the clock. His ears straining to the room. He wanted to hear if anything changed. After the first four hours, he could no longer keep the thoughts of his attack away. They had corroded his mental armour and found the space in the back of his mind where

112

he was doing his best to keep the ordeal. He cried openly and with such gut-wrenching sobs that he feared he would never be able to stop. He no longer cared about how dirty he was externally. His insides felt dirty. There wasn't a single part of him that hadn't been assaulted in this hellish place. He could feel embers of a buried rage beginning to ignite in his heart. Hour twelve saw him give over to the bonfire of rage in his heart. Wincing he stood up and roared his anger at the invisible attacker who had defiled him. He needed to punch something. To expel his rage through his fists and hurt something. Anything. His disgust and rage were consuming him and he needed to get it out. He punched the wall and the door. He kicked and slapped his face. Anything to express his current state. Hour sixteen saw him exhausted and curled up on the floor. His rage, while not sated, had given over to exhaustion. He drifted in and out of uneasy sleep. Every time he felt himself enter a dream state he started awake. He knew he couldn't trust his dreams. Instead, he lived in limbo, unaware of the tears that were slowly falling. Every part of him ached. His eyes were dry and sore. His rear was in agony. He was sure he was bleeding from there, but he refused to check for fear of confirmation. His knuckles were bruised and bloody. There wasn't a part of him that didn't ache with the same pain he felt in his heart.

After twenty-four hours, he had succumbed finally to panic and spent a full four fours screaming for help. This had yielded no results, bar leaving his throat sore and his voice hoarse. He knew that nobody was coming. He was truly alone, but he was convinced the silence would suffocate him. The only way to breathe was to scream. To shatter the thickness of the air. To remind himself that he was still here. He was present. He was broken but the slither of the fight he had left wasn't going to allow him to just give up. He paced the room until he grew weak, then sank to the floor in despair. Twenty hours had passed since he first looked at the clock. He was convinced now that it was mocking him. Time had taken a spongy quality with each movement of the hands he felt himself further unravelling. Now thirst and hunger had taken hold of him. He'd hoped that the room would feed him again or at least give him something to drink, but neither had happened. Alone, with no way out, he did the only thing he could think to – sleep. He knew he must allow himself to enter his dreams. It was the only way he could escape the room. Escape the hell he found himself in. Most of all, it let him escape his violated body even if it was only briefly. If something came and murdered him while he slept, then so be it. He had tried. There was no real fight in him anymore. He was empty of strength and desire to keep going.

There were no dreams at first, only darkness and a sense of floating until the nightmares started. They changed constantly; in one he had a knife sticking from his chest as Sarah cried for him, while in another, he was hanged, as an invisible assailant laughed. It was the same laugh that had attacked him in a different life. Its cold shapeless voice haunting him even here. He moaned in his sleep to an empty room. His mind trying to flee the dream and that laugh. He only managed to fall deeper into his dreams. In a third he was set on fire, the flames consuming him as he screamed and thrashed on the floor, the hungry pain licking every inch of him. The most recent involved his fingers being cut off by a faceless attacker. The sound of the blade crunching through the bone in his hand was too much and he forced himself back to the surface. Back to the room. Back to his body. He checked his hand was intact as he moaned his dissatisfaction at being back here. Slowly and with the groan of a man three times his age, Grant shakily got to his feet.

He had no reason to stand other than to change position in his prison. The room wasn't giving him up any time soon he feared. Glancing at the clock he realised that he'd been in a daze for over an hour since he had woken up. He'd been standing staring into space for the whole time without feeling the time pass. "I'm finally going fucking mad," he muttered to the silence. They were the first words he had spoken in what felt like days. He regretted the choice instantly as a fresh wave of pain came from his throat. Walking over to the door, he tried the handle again, but as he'd expected it refused to turn. He was too tired to rage at this or anything else. He was sore, he was hungry and beyond thirsty. His whole boy ached for rest and sustenance. The clock had been of no help to him. What did time matter when a minute lasted as long as it wanted? Time had taken on an elastic feel that no longer followed the rules.

"YOU FUCKING WHORE," a voice shrieked in his ear. Grant cried out in surprise. His body shuddered in fear and recognition. "No..." he whimpered. Tears started to gather in frantic eyes.

"YOU FUCKING WHORE!" the voice screamed again. Panic-fuelled, he tried the handle again, rattling the door, which refused to budge. "Please," he begged an invisible God as fingers he could not see dug into his shoulders and spun him around. Grant let out a scream of terror as he was forced to face the empty room. His bladder let a warm stream of urine out. He couldn't go through this ordeal again.

"You beautiful cunt." a deep male voice whispered in his ear. Grant was thrown across the floor, landing in a heap in the middle of the room.

He didn't have the strength to fight against the spectral hands that tore at his clothes. "You're a bad boy!" an ancient female voice croaked in his ear as his trousers were pulled down, exposing his rear once again. A chorus of laughter filled the room. "You beautiful cunt," a familiar voice whispered as his cheeks were once again pulled apart. Sobbing, Grant knew that it was futile to fight or resist. The wetness was spat onto his exposed opening again, but there was no warning this time. He screamed as a thick cold length was thrust into him with such force that he was moved two inches across the floor. The invisible predator remained indifferent to his screams.

The pain of the invasion was intense, cold and the intruding object was so large that he could feel things tearing inside him as his attacker increased the tempo of his assault. "You." Thrust. "Are." Thrust. "Mine." Thrust.

Grant lay on the floor, forcing himself once more to detach from his body and be free of the circumstances he found himself trapped in. He could feel the invisible eyes watching his ordeal. His tears fell silently and openly as his invisible assailant muttered vilely to itself. But they were just words. Words that the body wasn't paying attention to. It was abusing a husk. Grant had checked out of this ordeal. He remained as detached as he could. Refusing to believe what was happening to him for a second time. His body was numb; he'd achieved that, at least. With a final violent thrust that brought Grant crashing back into his body, it was over. He felt cold wetness inside him, and then a strange emptiness as his attacker pulled out of him with a chuckle. "You beautiful cunt," it whispered. An invisible hand caressed his buttocks.

He knew the room was empty now, even though he couldn't see anything. Alone with his shame, he pulled his trousers up, wincing. Tears continued to fall unnoticed as he slowly stood up, gasping in pain. He could still feel his attacker inside him, there was a warm wetness leaking from him which he refused to address. He knew deep down that it was blood. This attack had torn up more than his soul. Instead, slowly, he walked to the door.

With a shaking hand, he tried the handle, certain that now it would turn. He would escape this room with its ghosts and dreams, the smell of his own piss and defeat.

When the handle refused to turn, he screamed, battering the door with weakened fists. As he slid to the dirty floor he was certain he could hear faint laughter. Whatever this place was, it was winning. If he was being punished, he didn't know why. How could a man with no memory atone for sins he couldn't remember? With red eyes, he watched the clock. The slow turning of the hands reminded him that he had nothing but time to figure it out.

Hours passed and he did not move. The voices did not return, and in the silence that engulfed him, Grant finally gave up hope. By his calculations, he had been in this room for seventy-five hours.

He had never understood how slowly time could move. He was dehydrated and he knew that he was no longer thinking clearly. He also realised that while he could realise this, a small vestige of himself remained in the husk sitting on the floor waiting for death. From time to time, he tried to turn the handle of the door, but it refused to move. He could feel hysteria winning.

His eyes drooped shut. Sleep was once again trying to claim him, but he fought it, afraid of what would be waiting when he woke. It was a futile fight; his body was beaten and broken, and his mind was held together by the thinnest of strands. He shifted slightly, trying to summon the energy to stand, but was defeated again. As his head slumped forward and his breathing deepened, he escaped the room for a brief period.

His sleep was dreamless but deep. So deep that he didn't hear the door open and a young girl enters, the knife in her hand catching the dirty yellow light of the room. She glanced at the sleeping figure, remembering how he had saved her years before. The years had not been kind to him, she thought as she scanned the room and focused on the bloody writing on the far wall.

Don't Trust Yourself.

BOOK OF SARAH – BOOK FOUR

19th October

In the five years, I've been married to Michael, I never understood the power of freedom. It's been two years since I first stepped into the library and during that time I have come to realise the power of books as a way to escape anywhere. If being Mrs Burns has given me anything it's the gift of knowledge. Well, that and the ability to take an absolute beating and still make a roast dinner that very night.

I was never a smart girl in school – sure I'd coast by with standard grades and poor grades and on very rare occasions surprised myself and everyone else around me by getting great ones. It was always a chore though. An item on the checklist of life that everyone must cross off being entering the magical world of adulthood (some fucking world!). I had never thought of reading as something fun, or a hobby. Truth be told, I'd never really thought of reading anything that a teacher hadn't forced me to read and discuss.

Don't get me wrong, the few times I did venture into the literary universe I enjoyed it. But now that I've stepped into the adventures of others I've experienced things that I never dreamed I could. I sobbed when George had to kill Lenny while nursing my own broken fingers. I've been terrified by a clown in a sewer, although I couldn't scream because my jaw was fractured, and even travelled with a group of hobbits during a winter where I couldn't leave the house because of the bruises on my face. The last two years in the Burns household has been an adventure of bruises and broken bones. I might be sitting in the living room nursing a black eye, but my mind is with a man searching for a tower. I've been to worlds that sixteen-year-old me would never have cared existed. Now they're helping to keep me alive.

The last couple of years have shown me that I am stronger than I realised. That despite being a human punchbag, who has days when she can't get out of bed because her husband was too rough with her the night before, can pick up a small portal and escape the hell she's living in. The first few months of attending were rough; I made the mistake of spending a whole day reading about a mum and son held hostage by a dog. I lost track of time and forgot to clean the house or have tea waiting on the table when he got in. That resulted in my first late fine. Mainly because he beat me so badly that the left side of my face was so swollen that I couldn't open my eye and I was too embarrassed to leave the house.

I've been very careful since then. I couldn't cope if he took away the library card. These adventures are the only thing that is keeping me sane. I've been smart about it though – I've made sure I read books on cooking and DIY so I can keep on top of the house. I leave them lying around so he thinks that my library visits are benefiting him and the house. Naturally, Michael credits himself with the suggestion that I joined a library and he has certainly enjoyed the results of my new cookery skills. (I was tempted to get a book on poisons but figured that the police might trace it back to me so thought better about it.)

In a bout of what I can only imagine was guilt at the beating the week before that left me unconscious for an hour, Michael even bought me a book. Naturally, because of how his brain is wired it was a terrible book. Some virgin who got herself into an abusive relationship with a billionaire. I made it halfway through before giving up. If the guy hadn't been a billionaire, she would have been stuck in my life. Only the life of Mrs Sarah Burns doesn't come with a safe word.

20th October

Two more days and I get to go back to the library. I can hold off for two more days. I mean, I could go in today, I've finished my book, but it's a Wednesday and Jean works Wednesdays. Don't get me wrong – I like Jean. She's in her fifties, chubby and always passes me a boiled sweet or two from her purse. She keeps trying to get me to read some romance novels but the covers always put me off. I don't need a man with muscles, a shirt that's ripped open and long flowing locks. She even once tried to talk me out of loaning a book about a girl who survives a home invasion and has to go on the run (turns out she was right, that was a horrifying read and I'm never touching anything by that author again.) Jean's always happy to chat, and once she even bought me a coffee in the café attached to the foyer and offered to set me up an email. When she saw the look of confusion on my face she asked me if I know how to use the web. I told her that the only web I knew belonged to spiders and that I made sure there were none around my house. I thought it was a funny joke; she just looked at me with sad eyes and a hint of pity. Even now I can hear the sadness in her fake laugh. I've heard of the internet don't get me wrong. It was a poor attempt at a joke, but at the same time, I've never been online. Michael can barely spell his name so he has no reason to want to get a computer in the house. In the Burns household, we haven't quite embraced the future.

There's no way they don't know. I used to try and hide the bruises, but Michael won't let me buy makeup. "So you can look even more like a whore?" is always his reply if I ask. So there've been occasions where I've had to go with yellow bruises showing on my face or arms. To be fair, they never mention it and they all keep that look of pity from their faces. Most of the time anyway. I have to admit, though, it's more than the books. It's freedom. After the last miscarriage, Michael just never thought to lock the door again. I don't understand it, but I'm always going to be thankful. It's not a massive library, just a small local one but having somewhere to go, outside this prison, keeps me going in ways I can't explain. I could go anywhere, but I feel a sense of genuine freedom there that I need from time to time. It's a safe place, where I can indulge in conversation and adventures that I can't get anywhere else. At this point, the library has become my home from home. Only there I don't have to worry about being hospitalised. Or worse. Another thing I've learned as Mrs Burns: there's always something worse than what you thought was the worst. And it's usually just around the corner, waiting with a smirk.

21st October

He's been in a foul mood today. He's got a bug from work and keeps throwing up, which means that I've had no choice but to run around after him all day. I did worry yesterday when he came home early; my biggest fear is that they'll let him go and I'll be stuck with him twenty-four hours a day until he gets a new job. I have to admit, he looked awful; his hair was plastered to his head with sweat and his face was grey. There was a sickly-sweet smell coming off him and his skin was hot with fever.

Without even thinking, I went into wife mode. I gave him a glass of water and some paracetamol and put him to bed. Much to my surprise, he didn't argue. I walked behind him as he slowly climbed the creaking stairs, stopping to catch his breath. Once he'd shuffled into the bedroom, I took over: off came the work clothes, which were plastered to him. I made all the right noises, cooing here and soothing him there.

While I was fussing around and tucking him into the bed he looked at me with those deep blue eyes. Despite the curtains being drawn, a lazy light sneaked through them, making his eyes sparkle like sapphires. Maintaining eye contact, he gently took my hand and whispered: "I love you. I know I'm a hard man to love, but you're my world." Then he fell asleep. I stood there for ten solid minutes looking at him. I can't remember the last time he said anything like that to me. Certainly not since we got married.

I touched his forehead, whether or not in affection I don't know, and he was burning up. Maybe it had just been the fever talking, but for a few glorious minutes, I forgot that I hated him. I forgot that he once put a cigarette out on my bum for coughing while he smoked. I forgot about the beatings and the times he's forced himself on me. For a split second, I was reminded of a man I used to love, who I wasn't afraid of. But the years have changed us both. He's grown crueller and I've grown stronger. He's grown more vicious and I've adapted to cope. Time has pulled us both along the path, dragged us through the prison of his making and neither of us is that bright-eyed kid we were at the beginning. Five years can change who you are on a deeper level than a few wrinkles and the worry of grey hairs. I still think back to the girl who went to the bathroom on her wedding day and convinced herself the man she saw was the result of beer. She was young and didn't know better, but there are so many nights when I wish she had just run. Gone back to her parents who loved her and never looked back.

I'm tougher now, but I still flinch if he moves too quickly. I measure my toughness by my ability to survive and that's something I'm excelling at. I'm going to have a limp for the rest of my life after he broke my ankle and didn't let me go to the hospital for three weeks. He's taken my youth and my hope. Now I'm content with survival.

In true Michael fashion, when he woke up he was back to his normal self. He only slept for a few hours, his deep snores could be heard around the whole house. A reminder that he was in my space when I should be free. These were my hours of freedom he was taking away from me. I heard him stirring upstairs and decided to get him back on his feet. A cynical part of me thought it would get him back to work faster, while another part of me; well I guess the part that had been sleeping until he reminded me of the man he used to be, the man Sarah Matthews was head over heels for, wanted to look after him. I don't know which part won the battle, but all of me started making him something to eat.

I made him tomato soup and a slice of dry bread to see if that would settle his stomach a little. I went upstairs to find him lying naked in bed, just as I'd left him. Sweat glistened on his hairy torso and the room stank of it. I grimaced a little when I walked in and made a mental note to wash and change the bedding as soon as he got up. He looked wiped out, his blue eyes full of pity for himself. He watched me enter the room and sit on the side of the bed.

"You need to eat," I told him, I offered to bring him the food in bed, thinking that it might ease up any potential mood that he would get himself in.

"Fuck off," he replied in a familiar acidic tone. I sighed, rolled my eyes a little, walked back to the kitchen and put the hot bowl on the table. The man who had given me flashbacks to when I was Sarah Matthews was gone, replaced by the standard Michael once again.

He wasn't far behind me, scratching his arse as he walked into the kitchen. His body was soaked in sweat and I could feel the heat coming off him. He didn't say anything, but plopped down on the chair and began to eat the soup. Thankfully it had cooled enough for him to guzzle his way down.

"Don't eat so fast, you'll make yourself sick," I warned.

"Fuck off slag," he muttered darkly under his breath. However, he did slow down as he shovelled the soup into his hard hateful mouth.

I turned to put the kettle on and started to make a coffee. I could hear the spoon scraping the bottom of the bowl. When I heard him cough and retch, it felt like time slowed down. I turned as he heaved and brought the soup back up. Thick red liquid flooded out of his mouth. He coughed and coughed, vomiting more up. It splashed into the recently-emptied bowl and slopped across the table. The acidic smell hit me and I baulked. My own eyes started to water and I saw lumpy red vomit dripping onto my freshly washed floor.

"The fuck did you do to the soup?" he roared, pushing himself up. The table shook and fresh vomit splattered on the floor. He had *the* look in his eye. He felt bad, so naturally 'mean Michael' was here to make sure I suffered too.

I tried to tell him that I'd not done anything to the soup, that he'd just eaten it too fast, but before the words could even form, he slapped me across the face with the back of his hand. Spinning from the force of the blow, I spun, slipped in the vomit and fell to the floor. Warmth soaked into my rear as I landed in the mess. He looked at me and burst out laughing. In my revulsion, I forgot who I was dealing with.

"What the fuck, Michael!" I screamed. I slowly started to stand up.

He was no longer laughing. There was a moment of deadly silence. I'd finally done it; I'd been stupid enough to get myself killed. But at that moment I meant every syllable.

"The fuck did you say to me?"

I froze, my outburst ringing in my ears. I couldn't have answered if I wanted to: his fingers dug into my face. His thumb hooked under my jaw and forced me to address the angry God floating above me. The smell of vomit clung to my body.

"I asked you a question cunt," he spat. Literally: small flecks of spittle and vomit misted my face. I tried to move my mouth, but his fingers dug in deeper. All I could do was shake my head. Tears of fright readied themselves to fall, but I refused to give him the satisfaction.

His sweat had begun to mix with the smell of the vomit. He repulsed me. "You made me fucking sick," he spat as he pushed me away with a flick of his wrist. "You can't cook for shit, and now you're serving me poisoned soup." His eyes were wild. "Just remember Sarah, it might have been till death do us part but if I'm ever on the way out, you're fucking coming with me."

"I never. I swear." I cried. The tears were falling freely now. Mrs Sarah Burns is still a wimp at heart.

"Prove it."

I looked at him blankly, confused as to how he expected me to prove I hadn't tried to off him (the urge has been there before.) "There's no soup left, Michael." I had to say it slowly. Fear had slowed my brain and sped up my heart. "I swear. I didn't do anything to your soup. I just..."

He never let me finish my sentence. "Soup here," he informed me, calmly pointing towards his not so empty bowl. The two words hung in the air.

I looked at him. His eyes were full of burning rage and hatred. I slowly shifted my gaze to the bowl. A mixture of red and clear liquid half-filled the dish. Lazy tendrils of steam still drifted from it. Lumps of and chunks of unidentifiable matter floated in it. I retched as he got a spoon and shook my head.

"Please..." I hate that word. It's never done me any good. In the history of our marriage, I've said 'please' in every way possible. It's never helped. I normally don't ever lower myself to using it, but this wasn't like other times. This was about to cross a line. If I hadn't been so revolted by what he was suggesting I would have marvelled at the sheer fact that were lines left to cross.

"Eat. The. Soup," he ordered, passing me the spoon. He pulled out the kitchen chair like we were on a date and motioned for me to sit down. Trembling, shaking my head in disbelief, I got to my feet. Seconds that felt like hours passed between us. I was fixed to the spot. Michael came behind me. Almost gently leading me to the table and pushing me into the chair. "Just eat the soup, Sarah. Show me you didn't poison me." His voice was so soft, it was almost tender. I sat, stupefied by the events. He put the spoon in the bowl. A fresh wave of the odour hit me, and without thinking I turned to vomit. "Don't you fucking dare." he hissed. Closing my eyes, I did my best to calm my churning stomach, swallowing the bile that had flooded my mouth. "One spoon. Two, tops. Then I'll know you didn't do anything to me." He sounded far away as I stared at the bowl. I could see bits floating to the top. The repugnant smell wafted towards me. I shook my head, pleading with him with my eyes.

"Please," I begged. He just looked at me with his cold blue eyes. Shaking, I reached forward with both hands to pull the warm bowl closer. My stomach flipped, and I gagged. My hand betrayed me and reached for the spoon. "I can't Michael. Please," I cried. The tears were falling freely now. I've experienced fear and revulsion in my five-year marriage that people wouldn't believe. This was something altogether different.

"EAT THE FUCKING SOUP!" he screamed and slammed his fist down. In my fright, I dropped the spoon and it clattered to the floor, breaking the spell.

"No," I whispered.

At first, I didn't think he heard me. I slowly lifted my head and that was when it happened.

He snapped.

He lunged and grabbed me by my hair and, with a flick of his hand, wrapped it around his wrist. I screamed as he pulled me from the table, and slipped for the second time in his vomit. Pain seared my scalp as he tried to hold me upright by my hair, but gravity had a different idea and I ended up taking him down with me. I tried to scramble, but I couldn't get my limbs to obey. Michael recovered first and was on his feet before I even knew I was on the floor. "You're going to eat that fucking soup," he screamed at me. In two strides he had the bowl in his hand. the hysteria in his voice was contagious; my body finally obeyed me and I scrambled backwards, trying to get away from that damned bowl. I made it a third of the way across the floor before his barefoot landed in my stomach. Surprise and pain pushed the air out of me. He was like a towering god, furious at my refusing his rancid gift. I tried to leave my body, but my brain also betrayed me. Bowl in one hand, he reached down and grabbed my hair with the other. I wanted to scream, to thrash, to bite and scratch. I did none of those things.

"Eat," he hissed. He brought the bowl to my lips, bending over so that he could force the rim between my lips. The smell assaulted my nose and I gagged. Seizing the opportunity, he tipped the bowl and lukewarm liquid poured into my mouth. I coughed and spluttered. My stomach churned in way's I didn't know the human body could. Warning saliva flooded my mouth, yet miraculously no vomit came. I honestly think if I'd added my own fluids to the mix he would have snapped and killed me there. The murderous energy in the room was almost contagious. Refusing to swallow, I tried to pull back. He roared and tipped the bowl over me. The last bits of liquid coated my face in a fresh assault.

"Not worth the fucking effort," he said. I sat there, vomit burning my eyes, the taste in my mouth, the bowl's contents dripping from my face and hair. He looked at me in disgust. "Get this fucking cleaned up," he said, and just like that, he left the room and stalked towards the shower.

Some days, survival is easier than on others.

I sat there for a full thirty minutes, unable to process what had just happened to me. It wasn't until I heard Michael slam the bedroom door that I realised I was no longer on the kitchen floor. It wasn't the cold red liquid dripping off me, nor the suffocating smell, that brought me back to my body. It was the pain in my clenched fist where my knuckles had turned white around the handle of the knife.

Like I said, some days it's just enough to survive. I just don't know how much longer I can do this dance.

22nd October

I cut my hair today. It wasn't exactly a conscious decision, but I was walking back from the library. I had just taken out a book about folklore and witchcraft. I don't know why I chose it, but there was a picture of a strong-looking woman on the front and I could do with some of those in my life at the moment. Jean looked a bit confused, but she must have seen the bruise on the side of my face and decided against saying anything. She had *that* look in her eye, the look I hate. The "oh you poor thing" look. I'd normally think *fuck Jean* – harsh, I know, but there's only so many times you can be looked down on by people who don't know what's going on – but this time the thought didn't really cross my mind. I was still in a sort of daze from yesterday.

I didn't want to go home after leaving the library. I'd spent two hours cleaning the kitchen and ended up binning my clothes. It might not sound like much, but I don't have many clothes. Hell, I don't have many things I can call my own at all. Good job I'm not a material person I suppose.

I couldn't shake the smell of vomit. I knew it was in my head, but it was all I could smell this morning. Even after washing my hair three times, I could still smell it. I wandered around aimlessly, a book in my bag, enjoying the chill in the air. It wasn't raining yet, but you could tell winter was on its way. People bustled all around me, ignoring me as I wandered down the busy streets. I stopped outside a hairdresser and caught sight of myself.

The pale, gaunt woman staring back was almost unrecognisable. A chaotic mass of long brown hair hung as limp as my spirit. I hadn't been to a hairdresser for years, I'd just let it grow and now it was halfway down my back. I saw my reflection touch it. I'd never been chubby, always somewhere between a 12 and a 14, but the person who looked back at me looked almost skeletal. Underneath the dead eyes, framed by bruising, were bags so dark and large that I could have used them to pack for a midnight escape. It was the first time in a very long time that I had stopped and taken stock of Sarah Burns. She looked as pathetic and beaten down as she felt. A poor example of my sex in comparison to the woman on the cover of the book in my bag. Inside the shop, I saw some women laughing together, foil in their hair and wearing gowns, they appeared to be having a great time. Another woman sat under a dome hair drier, the look of sheer calm on her face was intoxicating. I thought of the woman on the book cover: she wouldn't be torn over simply walking into a shop and asking them to trim a little off the bottom. Sarah Mathews would have just walked in and started chatting to them. I'd spent years reading about powerful women, from Offred's unbreakable spirit to Dolores Claiborne finally taking matters into her own hands. I thought of Lisbeth surviving and Kitai charging forth and leaping in to save the day. Those were the women that should be making Sarah Burns. I've been a part of every one of their adventures. This was just another step forward. Before I knew it, I was inside the shop. The warmth hit me at once and I realised how cold I was. The nerves got the better of me a little as I took my coat off as I stood there for a second frozen, doing my best to ignore the voice of terror in my head. There was a moment where I nearly bolted, leaving my coat on the floor and dashing back out into the street. Before I could second-guess myself, or before my feet could carry me screaming back to my prison, a beautiful young woman had come over to me and smiled, doing her best to ignore the bruising on my face. She said something and I just nodded as she gently guided me towards an empty chair. The chattering continued around me, the sound of women, something I'd long forgotten.

She offered me a coffee as I sat down, averting my eyes from the wraith staring back at me from the mirror. When she came back with the drink, she told me that my stylist Shirl was going to be with me in a minute. "You'll love her," she beamed and walked away.

Oh, what a woman Shirley was. Easily six feet tall, and carrying a few extra pounds, but there was a warmth about her. Her accent was thick, even for Liverpool. "What yer 'avin, my love?" she inquired, running her fingers through my dry hair.

"Erm...." I froze. I didn't know what I wanted. I could feel tears welling up. I hated that he had got so under my skin. Even now, I could smell the vomit. "I... haven't been to the hairdressers in a long time," I said apologetically.

Shirley just laughed, a great big booming laugh. It was such a warm sound, with no malice in it. "Oh babe, I can see that. You've more split ends than a bag of snake tongues." The expression was so out of the blue that I couldn't help but laugh. "Than a what?" I asked still laughing.

"Oh, who the fuck knows. I just open me gob and roll with whatever falls out." Her warm eyes looked me over; they lingered for a moment on the bruise. "Lucky for you, old Shirley knows a thing or two about hair." She offered me a warm smile. "Now, your hair needs some serious TLC. I'm gonna get our Luce to give you a wash 'n deep condition while I go for a smoke, and then you and I are going to sort yer head out." She laughed that laugh again, went over to a skinny young girl, pointed over to me and then gave me a wink as she went out the back.

Luce spoke to me non-stop as she washed and conditioned my hair. I can't remember the last time someone touched me without there pain being involved. She spoke about the weather, her holiday, her friends and a night out she'd had at the weekend, her fingers tenderly massaging my scalp, the warm water washing off years of damage to my hair and to my soul.

A loud laugh announced the return of Shirley. "Right, queen. Let's get your head sorted!" She led me back to the chair. I sat back down, refusing to look at the woman in the mirror. I remembered now why I hated coming to hairdressers. I didn't want to have to see that weak woman staring back at me. Michael didn't like me to wear makeup unless we were going out somewhere (which was a rarity), so all I could focus on was the bruise on the side of my face. I could feel myself tensing back up, but before I could, Shirley spoke up, "So darlin', any thoughts on what to do?".

The creature staring back at me was gaunt and unloved; frail and weak, it could barely carve a space in the sun, let alone hope to come out the other side.

"I just want to change," I whispered

"We thinking a new style or just a little bit off – sort the ends out?"

"I'd like it short please."

"Oh, fabulous!" Shirley beamed, "How much are we thinking? It's a big step love – but as I'm always telling my girls, it's only hair. It'll grow back."

The tone of the conversation had changed; it was on the tip of my tongue, to ask for help, to confess to this stranger that I was in

Hell and couldn't escape. I could still smell the vomit. I could still feel his hand wrapped in my hair, forcing that.... that filth into me. A single tear fell down my cheek, my eyes were locked on the bruise. The realisation that the wraith was all that remained of Sarah Mathews was breaking the defences I had built up to survive.

"Short enough that nobody can grab it." My voice was barely a whisper, but silence descended on the salon for a second. Shirley looked at me. I half-expected her to say something funny, to diffuse the tension that I'd brought in with me.

Instead, she called over to Luce, whispered something in her ear and sent her off. Our eyes locked in the mirror. I was expecting 'the look', and a flood of pity for the poor battered wife. Instead, she looked at my cheek and said, very matter-of-factly, "I'll have you looking gorgeous in no time babe, and we'll make sure the bastard never grabs your head again." Luce came back over with a mug, I was confused and looked at the contents. It was full of wine. "A woman cutting her hair because she wants a new look is always emotional," Shirley stated with the wisdom her position offered her. "A woman cutting her hair so a man can't get her is a step in the right direction. I always want them to celebrate small victories. Now drink up and let Shirley do the rest."

That was the last she spoke of it. I could have brought it up again, especially as I drank the cheap wine. Instead, I found myself laughing with her as she spoke about "her one," who she said she wanted to murder daily, but was a good man. She never brought up the bruise. She cut my hair, slowly sectioning, trimming and then styling it. She kept everything light, everything friendly and above all, everything was about me.

After an hour she was done. I had kept my eyes downcast, not daring to look at the woman in the mirror. With a click, the hairdryer was turned off and she put some product on my refreshed hair. "Now, that is a badass chick I see in the mirror." Shirley declared.

Hesitantly, I looked up.

My hair was gone and with it, so was the wraith. Sarah Burns had finally had gone through her metamorphosis. The woman staring back was someone new. Whereas before it had been down my back, now it was cut close to my scalp. I'd been worried I would look like a boy, but Shirley had made me…. Beautiful. She had styled it like a twenties woman of note. I had a small curl at the front and the sides were slicked back. "It'll only take you a few minutes to sort out in the morning," she beamed, "and if you need to make a quick getaway, it's short enough that….well, let's just say there's very little to get a hold of."

I was lost for words. Turning my head from side to side, admiring her work. I ran my fingers over my head, "Shirley… thank –" but she cut me off before I got a chance to finish.

"I'm only going to say this once – you're not the first woman or even the hundredth one I've had in that chair who wanted shorter hair." Her eyes burned with passion. "But if I don't say this, it'll play on my mind all night. I don't know what your story is. I'm not going to pretend to. But you came in here and you chopped that hair off. Whether you believe it or not, whether you even know it or not, you just took a step away from the bastard. Whatever brought you in here, whatever made you think that it was time to chop your wig, keep listening to it hun. And if that voice tells you to run – you listen. You fucking run. Men are beasts at the best of times. Some of them are like a puppy. Give them a good meal and a good lay and they treat you like the boss. Some of them though, well, some of them are like wild dogs. They'll rip you down just to get the marrow from your bones. A man who's willing to let his woman walk around with a mark like that on her face, well, that's a man who knows he's close to the marrow. The second they smell the main course, they'll do what they can to get to the meal. Just remember that." She got me my coat and waved away any payment, telling me that it was her good deed for the week. She hugged me deeply, her warmth and personality healing some of the cracks in my heart. I know I'll never go back there again, but something changed in me. I felt a sliver of strength come back to me.

He never even commented on the hair when he came home to his tea. He looked at me, grunted, ate his food and skulked into the living room to watch the football. His anger was palpable, I saw his fists clench, but something about me made him change his mind.

After I'd done the dishes I took my book out of my handbag and settled down to read for a spell. It took me a second to realise that I had the same haircut as the woman on the cover.

23rd October

I did something today. Something so wrong and exciting and against everything I thought I could do that I'm still not entirely sure what happened to me. I'm getting ahead of myself, but I'm going to remember this date for as long as I live. (Which let's face it, with my life might not be as long as I'd like).

After I got Michael up and off to work this morning, I sat in the kitchen. I do that sometimes – it's easy to just get lost in there. When you feel like someone's property, sitting with the utensils can seem right. But this was something else. Shirley's warning was running around my head.

I can't smell the vomit anymore, which is a good thing. I don't smell it in the house and, even better, it isn't following me around. Sure the house smells of bleach, but at least that smell has gone. I don't even feel dirty now. As soon as I left the hairdressers yesterday, I noticed I couldn't smell it. I read another chapter of the book. I know it's not real, but it's full of tales of these witches, Gods and other deities. All female. All with a tragic story of how a man damaged them, but they still sought greatness. They evolved past the hurt, brushed away the tears and managed to rise to the pantheon of powerful women who have been erased from history.

That could be you, my mind whispered.

I paused, cup halfway to my lips. I'd had a positive thought about myself. It felt so alien, but it was there, like a buzzing in my ear. I went to run my fingers through my hair, a common action for me when I was nervous or thinking. I'd forgotten that I'd had it all chopped off. That was when it dawned on me. Today I am a different woman than I was yesterday.

I won't lie; I wish Michael had said something about my hair. Good or bad, it would have at least been nice to have felt seen. It would be easy to attribute it to Michael being an arsehole, but I think that's just men. I remember once, years ago, Mum dyed her hair blonde (brown hair runs in the family), and it took Dad three days to notice. Oh, she hit the roof when he finally said something. It hurts me to think of them sometimes. Little memories like that can hurt more than any punch. The little optimistic girl they raised was so eager to be a wife that she didn't take into account how much of herself she would be losing. The girl who spent her wedding day talking herself into overlooking behaviour that would become standard in her marriage. I could scream when I think of her. I could feel the familiar tendrils of maudlin despair creeping out of the floor to drag me down.

Before I even knew what I was doing, I was showered, dressed and walking to the library. I just needed to get out of the house and escape the tendrils. They'd still be waiting when I got home, but for now, I was enjoying the crisp autumn air. It was a 'Grant-Day' so I knew he would be there. I guess, deep down, I just wanted to look into those deep brown eyes, so full of warmth and compassion. I practically skipped all the way there.

He wasn't at the desk when I walked in. I scanned the floor but couldn't see him. Jean was on the counter and looked right past me – I don't think she recognised me, which just made me feel even better about the new hair.

I spotted him by the children's books. He was talking to a pretty young woman with a gorgeous little girl. I hate to admit this, but for a split second, I was jealous. How ridiculous is that? I have no right to him; he doesn't belong to me, but watching her giggle and run her fingers through her hair, touching him lightly on his broad chest, I wanted to run over and punch her in the face. I could see it so clearly, hear her bones crunching under my fist as I marked my territory.

With a little shake of my head, I came back to reality. What was I doing? I was a married (*owned*) woman. Why was I here, getting jealous of a woman I barely knew? Silently, I made a move towards another section of the library before I turned my daydream into a reality. After I turned away, I had to force myself to relax my fists. I hadn't even realised I'd clenched them. I found myself browsing through the religion section, looking for something else with inspiring women. I found one: *Celtic Lore & The Women Who Shaped It*. I couldn't leave empty-handed, so decided to take another chance and get this out. I never leave without something, and this would make a nice addition to the one at home, at least until I had to bring them back, but that would just be another excuse to leave the house and see Grant. Walking to the desk, book in hand, I was brought out of my daydream by someone calling my name. I turned and there he was. I felt my rage melt into something light and hopeful. "Hi, Grant," I whispered, trying to control the blushing.

"Wow. Look at you!" he beamed. His whole face lit up, eyes wide with wonder. "You got a haircut! Well obviously, I mean you know you got it cut. I mean. Wow. Look at you. Just… wow."

I was blushing so deeply I could feel the heat coming from my face. He continued to ramble for a few more minutes; I nodded and smiled, thanking him for the kind words. He walked with me to the counter, we made polite small talk, but I caught him snatching glances at me. He was smiling the warmest smile I've ever seen in my life. A smile I was returning.

"Listen," he said, taking a deep breath, as he processed the book, "I finish in about twenty minutes. I'd love to go for coffee. With you. If you want. I mean… if it's weird..."

He let the words hang in the air, trying not to let his gaze linger on my wedding ring. Sarah from three days ago would have muttered something and fled, never to return. Sarah from two days ago would have made an excuse and gone home to daydream. Sarah from yesterday would have stammered, run away and cried in the toilets. I'm not sure who I am now, but I am not that girl from three days ago or the woman I was yesterday.

Before I could overthink it, my mouth did the work for me.

"Sure. That would be nice, Grant." I smiled my best smile and, I swear, he started to blush. "I'll just go wait," I said, pointed to the seated area and smiled.

Those were the longest twenty minutes of my life.

We went to a small coffee shop around the corner, only a few minutes walk away, and the conversation flowed. The coffee was bitter, but the company, oh, the company was sweet.

We spoke about nothing of importance, but he made me laugh. I can't remember when I last laughed at a joke. My face hurt from smiling, muscles that I think I'd forgotten how to use suddenly remembered their purpose.

"You look really pretty when you smile," he stated, after a joke, I can't remember. As soon as the words were out of his mouth he blushed. "I'm sorry, that was, well that was pretty forward of me. I mean you're pretty all the time." His mouth dropped open as if his brain had caught up with what he was saying. "I mean... sorry. I shouldn't be saying that."

He was practically beetroot, and I think my face matched his. Years with Michael had left me ill-equipped to take a compliment. I muttered a 'thank you' and swiftly changed the subject. I saw him look at my wedding ring three times, then he looked at the bruise on my face. Each time his mouth opened to say something about the ring or the bruise I'm not sure, but he had enough sense to not broach the subject. As strong and confident as I was feeling, that would have been too much for me. I don't think I'll ever be strong enough to talk about that part of my life.

The closest he got was after our second cup of the bitter coffee. (I'll say it now: I'm not a fan of whatever a cappuccino is. I think I'll stick to my Nescafé. Still, it's something that I can say I've tried now.)

"Would you like a slice of cake?" he asked as he stood to order another cup. I looked at my watch and realised I'd have to get home soon. My day release was coming to an end and prison was waiting.

"I best not. I've got to be getting home."

"Oh. Course. Sorry. Mr Sarah's going to be waiting for you, I imagine." He sounded a little glum, but I burst out laughing. *Mr Sarah.* My word – I could just imagine Michael's face at hearing that. Glancing at Grant's face, I saw he clearly didn't get the joke and felt a little mean. I didn't want him to think I was laughing at his expense. I shook my head, lightly. "No, not waiting. But I've still got a few chores left to do, I'm afraid."

"Well, next time we'll make sure and get a cake. If you want. Sorry. That was quite presumptuous of me."

"Which? That we'll get cake?" My heart was beating so hard in my chest I'm surprised it didn't knock the cups off the table.

"No," he whispered, beetroot once again. "That there will be a next time."

My throat went dry. I was at a crossroads. He was a sweet man: I could have seen that even if I'd had no eyes. But I was married –

to a bad man, sure, but if I went for a second coffee, a second date (was that even what this was?) no good could come from it. I could feel my heart beginning to break.

"What cake?" I shocked myself by saying. I'd been planning to agree that there wouldn't be a second time, that I couldn't do this. But the smile on his face was enough to light even the darkest of nights.

"Well, I guess that depends on what your favourite cake is. If we're stealing moments, we should make them count."

That was it; we were officially co-conspirators. Here I was, stealing my first moment of happiness in years, and I finally had someone who seemed to understand what that meant for me.

It was an afternoon of firsts for me. Since the day I became Mrs Sarah Burns, I'd not once been asked what my favourite anything was. I couldn't even think what my favourite cake was.

"Carrot cake," I replied, thinking back to being young and my nan bringing her homemade cake out of the kitchen. "My favourite cake is carrot cake." Even as I said it I could feel the love of my family from the past. The cake was more than a treat from my nan, it was a token of her love for me. She wasn't a big cake person, but she knew I loved it, and that was enough for her. I needed more moments like that in my life. If I could get a memory like that with Grant, I'd be a happy woman.

His smile widened, "Then next time we'll make sure and get that with the first cup."

We left not long after that. He went to hug me, but when he did I flinched and he withdrew. Sometimes the damage is so deep in someone you don't even know it's there. Grant saw a glimpse of it, but he didn't flinch. He took a step back, smiled and said that he'd see me soon. We didn't set a date so I don't know when. But I know one thing. I'm really looking forward to that carrot cake.

25th October

He's sleeping upstairs. It's just gone 3.00 a.m. I've got to get him up in a few hours, but I haven't been able to sleep all night.

I made it home in time to rustle up a quick tea and have a bath run for him when he came in. He looked at me in the hallway when he came in, suspicion in his eyes, but nothing passed his lips; he grunted and went up for his bath.

We ate in silence. He kept stealing glances at me: I pretended not to notice, but I caught every single one. Twice he went to say something but choked on the words. I could feel knots tightening in my stomach. I was convincing myself that he knew where I'd been. That he'd been spying on me. His all-seeing eye capturing my betrayal. Part of me, though, relished the secret. I had defied him and his rule over my heart, albeit for a few innocent hours. Sarah Matthews wasn't as dead as I thought she was. She'd just been hiding.

After tea, I did the dishes in silence, mentally replaying the afternoon. Dreaming of the slice of cake I was going to have. Wondering if Grant's lips were as soft as they looked. I've never thought of a man as anything other than a brute since my wedding day. That's all I've known men to be in matters of love. Yet with Grant, there's something more, there's a gentleness to him. I was so lost in thought that I never even heard Michael come into the kitchen. He must have been standing there for a good five minutes before he cleared his throat. I jumped and turned around.

"I've run you a bath."

I paused trying to think of the last time he did something like that for me. Of the last time, he did *anything* for me.

The confusion on my face must have been plain; he tried to smile, and I saw a glimmer of the man I once loved, a thin shred of the boy who made me laugh and told me I was the prettiest girl in the world. "Nice to know I can still surprise you."

I could almost hear Sarah Matthews screaming not to trust him. "Oh, you certainly can do that," I said, bitterly. His smile faltered for a split second; when it came back, the boy I loved once was gone. It was Michael again. Michael acting.

"Thanks though. I'll go have a soak with my book." I paused, worrying that this might be a trap. "If that's okay with you?"

"Course. I wouldn't have offered if it weren't." He forced his smile wider. It had an ominous edge to it, but I know him well enough; he's forgotten how to smile. What a miserable pair we make. I slunk past him.

By the time I got out of the bath, my skin pink and soft, he was waiting in the bedroom. I sighed inwardly, knowing what was about to happen. The bath suddenly made sense.

I tensed as I walked around the side of the bed, waiting for the expected pull towards him. But it never came. I quickly got dressed for bed, body stiff with tension, all the relaxation I'd experienced in the bath evaporating.

"I know we've had a rough few years of it love," he began. I turned to face him. "But I do love ya." I searched his face and saw that he really did believe it. He thought the things he did to me were an act of love. I couldn't tell where the trap was, but I knew there was one coming. I couldn't think of what to say. I know I should have told him that I loved him too, but at this point, why bother lying?

He was going to do whatever he was going to do, and my offering a fake declaration of love wasn't going to change that. He nodded a little, obviously thinking along the same lines. "I said the other day, and I'll say it again. I know I can be a hard man at times. I know I'm not the easiest man to get along with. I've got...issues." He paused. I looked him in the eyes. No: I locked eyes with him. I could feel a small fire burning inside me. A small sliver of strength, but enough to look him in the eyes and not turn away. Whatever was coming, I'd face it head-on.

"But we were good once." he continued, then corrected himself. "*I* was good once. Your hair. Fuck me, Sarah, you look gorgeous. I should tell you more, but after everything, you know, the drink and losing the baby."

I felt my heart turn to stone. A thousand words of hate flooded my mouth and I had to physically bite down to keep them in.

"Well," he said, "I guess what I'm trying to say is, well, ah fuck, you know I'm no good at this shit." He fake-laughed, trying to diffuse the tension in the room. "I mean, fuck, I'm just going to say it. You look so different now. Stronger I guess. Gorgeous, I mean. Ah, I'm rambling. I'm just going to say it."

"Michael..." I whispered, suddenly terrified. I didn't want to know whatever had brought about a change like this in the man I'd grown to hate. Whatever could make him behave like this towards me could never be good. But, true to form, he ignored me.

"I want us to have another bash at it," he said.

I was lost. Not that I've ever known where I was going in this marriage. I've learned I can take a beating. I've learned you can run for years on empty. But to see him so unsure of himself, to see him reduced to a lost little boy, that filled me with a terror deeper than anything I've ever felt before.

"Another bash at what?" I whispered.

"Oh, you're shaking. Jesus, what a man I must be to make you shake like that." Before I knew it, he was up off the bed and had an arm around my shoulders. He sat us both down on the edge of the bed. "I want us to try for another baby, Sarah. I think you're strong enough for it. I mean, you know, I'll be good this time. I won't stress ya. I'll stop the drinking. Let's do it. Let's, you know – let's try again. Second time lucky eh?"

I felt sick but nodded. Why did I nod? Why didn't I say no? Why didn't I scream and fight and tell him that he was the reason my heart was broken beyond repair, the reason I didn't have a daughter? I have never hated him more than I did at that exact moment. "You look so strong now, Sarah," he whispered and leaned in to tenderly kiss my neck, oblivious to the fact that my skin was actively trying to crawl from my body. He didn't wait for me to reply, which just meant that Michael had decided for me: we were having a baby.

I went through the motions. I will give him some credit, he was gentle. He tried to be tender, he tried not to hurt me and when he shot his dirty load inside me, he looked me in the eyes and told me he loved me. If I'd had a knife to hand I would have buried it in his back at that moment. He fell asleep not long after and I lay there.

I could feel his seed inside me, cold and wet. I could imagine it crawling towards my womb. I tried to imagine a wall that would stop him from getting me pregnant. Stop his dirty horrid little swimmers completing their unwelcome journey. He called me strong; he finally realised that I've cut my hair then. If this is the change in him, it's too late.

And all I can hear is what Shirley said: "A man who's willing to let his woman walk around with a mark like that on her face, well that's a man who knows he close to the marrow. The second they smell the main course, they'll do what they can to get to the meal".

Well, Michael might not know it yet, but the buffet is closed.

<u>Chapter Five</u>

Grant awoke with a start; the pain quickly followed. He realised that he was lying on a dirty floor. Before he could take full stock of his surroundings everything came flooding back. The slow passage of time, the thirst, the madness that had been gnawing at his sanity. With aching muscles, he pushed himself into a sitting position. His throat burned, desperate for hydration and his stomach cramped with hunger pains. The urge to close his eyes, give in to the inevitable oblivion that was just around the corner was almost too much to resist.

"Thank God," a young female voice sighed. "I thought you were never going to wake up."

Turning towards the source of the voice, he saw a young woman, no older than sixteen, sitting cross-legged across from him. Her pale skin looked like it had never seen the sun. Her brown hair hung limp and greasy. He looked into her cautious eyes as she spoke: "I tried to wake you, but you were out for the count." With a fluid movement that didn't seem to fit with her thin frame, she stood and crossed the room to him.

Dumbfounded, Grant tried to speak, but a dry croak came out instead. Pity crossed the girl's face. "Save your energy."

Extending her hand, she helped him to his feet. The room spun and he nearly went down again. She helped him regain his balance. "Wow," she said. "They've done a number on you." Tears sprang to Grant's eyes; the power of human contact was almost too much. He didn't have the energy to wipe them away. "What's going on?" Grant whispered, unashamed of his display of emotion.

"I have no idea," she replied, "but it looks like you've had a rough ride of it since we last met."

It took him nearly a full minute of uncomfortable staring before he could place her. "You're the kid!" he half-cried, half-whispered, throat burning from use before it dawned on him. She was much older than the last time he had seen her "How long have I been in here?"

"I don't know. I just came in and found you on the floor." Darkness threatened to claim him again. Nothing made sense, and he was weak with confusion and hunger. "But...you..."

"Listen, don't try and make sense of it. Nothing makes sense here. Half of me thinks I've been wandering the rooms for about six years. Like, I remember you saving me from that thing years ago and at the same time, it feels like yesterday." She paused, cocked her head as if she heard a noise, licked her lips and carried on, "The other half of me thinks I've only been here a few days. I woke up in a room just like this one and don't remember anything about how I got here. I just know my name. I'm Siân, by the way." She looked at him plainly, brown eyes glistening sickly in the dirty light. Her long brown hair hung limp, framing her thin face. "And you are?"

"Grant," he whispered.

"Well, Grant, what do you say we go through the door and see what's in the next room?" She motioned to the open door.

The invitation hung in the air. He felt a small kindling of hope: after so many unknown days and hours, he was no longer on his own. "If you could decide quickly, Grant, that would be great. Your penmanship has totally creeped me out." She nodded towards the bloody writing on the wall. Following her gaze, Grant read the message: *Don't Trust Yourself.*

"I didn't do that..." he whispered, horrified.

"You sure?" Siân replied, the uncertainty clear in her voice, and stole a glance at his hands.

Raising his hands in front of his face, he was confronted with blood-coated fingers. Two of his nails had been ripped off. The blood had crusted thickly. There was no pain, but he had no memory of writing anything. All he could do was shake his head. He knew that he'd come close to madness while locked in the room but genuinely believed that he'd been aware of every painful minute. The idea that there were missing memories of his actions here scared him on a deeper level. *What if it used you again* his mind whispered as a wave of panic crashed into him.

160

Using mental strength he didn't think he had anymore Grant shoved the thought down as deep as he could in his mind. He would not let this girl see the pain the assault had caused him. That would be staying here. The person he used to be already eluded him; the memories he'd created in this place were all he currently had to hold onto. If he didn't have those, then he didn't know if he *could* actually trust himself. Maybe the message was accurate.

"Come on," the girl said. "This room gives me the creeps." With that, she strode confidently across the room and through the open door. Grant followed, with a parting glance at the writing on the wall. He noticed that the clock had disappeared.

Neither he nor Siân flinched when the door shut behind them of its own accord. The effect had grown tired for both of them. He scanned his surroundings, to see where his nearest exit was. There were two doors this time. Like a lost lamb, he looked to Siân for guidance. He could feel an energy coming from her; there was something about her that, despite her youth, provided him comfort. The last room had broken parts of him that he was unsure could ever be fixed; he had been violated in a way that had shattered the little fighting spirit he had. Right now, he needed to follow someone; he felt no shame at admitting that to himself. If he could just be led for a bit, he was sure he could get some of his spirit back. His mind was working triple time, trying to build him back up now he wasn't alone, trying to erase the bitter memory of his attack and trying to convince himself that he wasn't in danger now. This girl had survived here for much longer than he'd been in here. Maybe she would bring him luck. Maybe -

"Oh, a double room," she said calmly, ripping Grant from his thoughts. "What way are you thinking?" she said, turning to look at him.

He just shrugged, still not fully alert. "I had a friend who used to say when in doubt, go left." He'd said it without thinking; for a second, he felt a memory come close to the surface, but when he tried to remember who the friend was, it drifted away like smoke. He was too tired to explore the memory fully. He let it sit like oil on the water of his mind. When he felt a bit more rested, he would drag it back to shore and study it fully. For now, he was happy with having company.

"Left it is then." She smiled confidently and strode across the room. As she put her hand on the doorknob, Grant's stomach knotted in pain. Thin, acidic water poured from his mouth. There was nothing solid in the liquid – he hadn't eaten in days – but its bright green colour still shocked him. Tears burned his eyes. Again he heaved and more liquid spilt out of him. He felt the girl's thin hand rubbing his back. The warmth of human contact gave him a little more strength.

Slowly, the pain in his gut subsided. His throat was on fire. He shakily wiped at his wet eyes, looked at the puddle on the floor and shuddered. Standing back up, he looked apologetically at the girl. She smiled wanly. "Don't worry about it." She turned to the doors again. "I say we go through the right door. If you reacted like that to me touching the left, I'm going to take it as a bad sign." She strode over and, before he could protest, opened the right-hand door.

There was no concern on her face, no lingering fear. For a split second his envy of her was all-consuming. He wished he had her confidence, her lack of fear of what horrors might be waiting in this room or the next. She wasn't bogged down by the weight of her experiences. She hadn't been *used* by this hell as a plaything. He could practically smell his shame filling the room.

"C'mon," she said gently, spurring him into action. "You'll like this room." A smile spread across her face as she went through. Grant sped across the empty room, close to panic at the thought that the door might slam shut before he made it through. He couldn't be alone again.

The new room's walls were off-white, the paint peeling in various degrees, showing a patchy grey underside. There were no windows, the dirty wooden floor was covered in various bits of debris and rubbish. Leaves, broken glass and wrappers sat unmovingly and covered in a thin layer of dirt. Grant was happy to note there was no writing on the wall and this room didn't stink of his urine or vomit. A single bulb hung from the ceiling, casting a sickly white light all around, adding depth to the shadows on the floor. But in the middle of this room was a large wooden table, and on it was, for lack of a better word, a feast. Joints of various meats of various sizes lay on platters. Fresh fruit and colourful vegetables were piled high in bowls. There were pitchers of what appeared to be fresh fruit juice. Crystal clear pitchers of water. Cuts of meat. Grant spied fragrant kinds of rice and freshly-baked loaves of bread. The scent of the food filled the room; saliva flooded his mouth and his stomach growled at the feast before him.

A shocked laugh escaped his dry lips, and Siân smiled. "The good thing about wherever we are – it always provides when you need it to the most."

Grant kept silent about what this place could do to you. He didn't know what she'd seen in her time here, and this didn't seem the time to regale her with his tales of woe. He could still feel that thing inside him if he didn't focus his mind elsewhere. His excitement at the food diminished almost instantly. As if sensing his change in mood Siân put her hand in his and nodded towards the feast. He felt the corners of his mouth twitch in an involuntary smile.

Together they approached the table, Siân reaching out first to grab a chicken leg, tucking into it with unashamed hunger. Taking his cue from her, Grant reached for a pitcher of water. There were no glasses, so he drank directly from the opening at the top. He couldn't remember drinking anything so refreshing. He had only planned to sip a few mouthfuls, fearful of upsetting his stomach again; four gulps later, he'd abandoned this notion completely. Hunger took over and, with a belch, he set about the food with gusto.

Siân didn't pause, moving on down the table; occasionally she'd suggest he try something she was eating. Smiling his first genuine smile since he arrived, Grant obliged her. Everything he ate tasted better than the last. Soon he felt his stomach was full to the limit, and he could eat no more.

Looking over the remains of the food, he saw that, between them, they had barely dented the feast. Siân seemed to be slowing down as she shovelled a slice of chocolate cake in her mouth. With raised eyebrows, she nodded towards the two-tier cake, which had a large chunk missing. Grant shook his head, unable to eat another bite. Taking a pitcher from the table, he walked slowly to the far wall. With a groan, he lowered himself to the floor.

"That was… just what I needed," he said softly.

"Agreed," Siân replied, taking rolls from a plate in the centre. "But who knows when we are going to get another meal." He watched as she put three rolls in each pocket, then tossed a couple to him. Snatching them with lazy ease, he placed them on his lap. "I'm stuffed," she said with a sigh and came to join him. "I don't know about you, but I could just go for a nap." Nodding, Grant could feel comfortable sleepiness creeping over him.

"The rooms like this are normally safe," Siân said with authority. "You know, the ones where you get given stuff. I've not had many of them, but when the room gives you a gift, it's usually given in abundance."

"How long have you been here for?"

"Honestly? I have no idea." she yawned, stretching her thin arms. "It feels like a few days but in the same way, I kind of feel like I've always been here."

"Do you not remember before? Your parents?"

"No. I just woke up here. I knew my name, and that was it. But I was just a kid. My first few days here, I just wandered around crying." He saw a change in her, the child she once was showing through. "I was such a baby." A hardness crept into her voice, pushing the child back into the shadows.

"I'll be honest – my first day here, I cried as well," he confessed. She gave him a smile that was older than her years. "I don't remember who I am either. I didn't even know my name."

"But you do now."

He nodded, "I do now."

"I remember you saving me, then everything after that's a bit of a blur." She was picking at her clothes. "You saved my life."

"Anyone would have done the same. I just wish I knew where we were."

"I've stopped questioning it. It just hurts my brain." She yawned again. "I'm going to have a sleep."

"I'll keep watch." He didn't mean the edge that crept into his voice.

"Nah. Just get some sleep. There's nothing better than a nap after food. I think. I mean, my experience is limited but I'm a simple kid," she said sleepily as her eyes shut. "Thank you, Grant." She put her head on his shoulder. The human contact was calming.

He had many questions for the girl, but she was already snoring lightly, and her warmth was giving him the energy and comfort he'd been craving since he'd arrived wherever this was.

Getting comfortable, he allowed himself a minute to take stock. He was alive. He was fed. He was no longer alone. Whatever this place was, it hadn't beaten the kid and, despite the horrors he'd faced, it still hadn't beaten him.

Or so he told himself. He understood, on a deeper level, that he was probably in denial. He still felt dirty from his assault; the mere memory of it made him sweat. He was trying his best to ignore the fear that they would get trapped in this room together. He might be alive, but he couldn't push his memories away.

Glancing at the girl sleeping on his shoulder, he felt a renewed sense of purpose. He didn't know who he was before he came here, but right now, he would take on the role of protector. The kid had survived alone, he had survived alone. He would get them out of here if it was the last thing he did.

Despite Siân's suggestion, sleep was the last thing he wanted to do. Yet despite his determination to stay awake, he was asleep before he had a chance to wonder if he'd aged as much as Siân had since they'd last seen each other.

He was running down a long hallway. Something was behind him. He knew he couldn't turn round for fear of slowing down. Whatever was behind him knew him well. It knew what he had done. (what have I done?) *He felt remorse, but he had been left no choice.*

He could hear her voice everywhere. The blood on his clothes was still wet and his t-shirt was sticking to him. (it's not my blood). *He reached a fork in the hallway. Two identical ways were open to him; should he go left or right? Without thinking he turned down the left hallway.* (When in doubt. go left) *Its old wallpaper was peeling and sparse. He could smell the decay all around him. His bare feet were near silent on the dark wooden floor. Something grabbed hold of the back of his neck. Ice-cold fingers scratching at the base of his skull.*

*A scream escaped him as he found an untapped reserve of
energy. He could see a door in the distance, but as he tried to
guess the distance his foot went out from underneath. Tumbling
to the floor, he knew death would be upon him any second.*

Someone was shaking him gently, calling his name. Slowly, he
returned to the waking world. Siân's hazel eyes greeted him, and
she smiled. "You're such a heavy sleeper!" she mock scolded.
He stretched with a groan and looked around. The table was
gone, the room was bare. "Looks like the buffet's closed," he
yawned.

"Good thing we took some to go isn't it?" Siân replied, patting
her pockets, "You sleep okay?" She was looking at him with
genuine concern.

A cold shiver crept down his spine and he brushed the imaginary
fingers from the base of his skull. "Bad dreams, I think." he
groggily replied. He rose to his feet, wincing as he stretched his
back. "I think I was being chased". He shook his head to let Siân
know that was all he could recall. "So – ready to move onto the
next room?"

"Yeah. Once the food goes, it's usually time to move on."

"That's a pretty good rule to live by, my friend," he chuckled,
despite the knot in his stomach, as they walked through the door.

They were in a large room. The walls were off-white, the paint peeling in various degrees, showing a patchy grey underside. There were no windows, the dirty wooden floor was covered in various bits of debris and rubbish. Leaves, broken glass and wrappers sat unmovingly and covered in a thin layer of dirt. "Oh look. We're back where we started," Siân remarked dryly. Grant wished he had some words of comfort to offer, but, coming up short, he stayed silent.

Once inside the room, the door slammed shut behind them. Neither of them paid any attention to this. There was no obvious way out. The walls, despite their aged appearance, were smooth and doorless.

Grant noticed that there was a book in the far corner. In the sparse environment, your eye couldn't miss it. Slowly walking over, he picked it up.

"What you got there?"

"I think it's a photo album," he replied, opening the thick cover. Inside were photos of a woman he didn't recognise. One of her as a child, holding a doll, her brown hair tied in a ponytail, grinning an innocent grin to whoever was taking the picture. In the next she was a young woman of sixteen, her green eyes sparkling with mischief. She stood over a cake that had "Happy Birthday" written on it in pink icing. in another, she was in a uniform, writing all over her shirt, a smile of pure joy on her face.

Siân had walked over to join him. "She's pretty," she commented as they looked through the photos. The woman was radiant in all the pictures. Dark hair, cascading down her shoulders, various outfits, progressing through her childhood until the last one. She stood, tall and slender, a white wedding dress hugging her slender frame. It was a simple gown, but her beauty added radiance to it. Her smile was the most genuine one he had seen. She was a girl, about to embark on a woman's journey.

"That's the last one," Grant said. There was no writing in the book, no clue as to who the woman was. "Look familiar to you?"

"Never seen it before. You?"

"I don't think so."

"Strange. Very strange." Siân looked up and scanned the room. Grant did the same. No doors had appeared. "Well, whoever she is, I hope she's not stuck in here with us."

Grant nodded in agreement. He wouldn't wish this hell on anyone. The effect of the short-lived respite in the previous room was rapidly fading. Putting the book under his arm, he did a lap of the room, running his hands along the dusty wall. "Now what? We wait?" He wasn't really asking, more just breaking the silence.

"Guess so," the girl replied. "Let's look at the photos again." Grant walked over to her, opening the book once more.

"She looks so happy," Siân remarked as they flicked through the first few pages. "Like, there's a kid who knows what it's like to be loved." A single tear fell from her eye.

"Siân? What's wrong?"

The girl's face crumpled and she began to sob. Wrapping his arms around her, Grant pulled Siân close. "I just want to go home," she sobbed. "I don't know where it is, but I want to be there." He pulled her close to him, he felt her relax into his hug, "I just want my mum" she whispered.

He held her as she cried, his own emotions whirling in his mind. He needed to say something to help her through this; she was shaking as she tried to quiet her sobs. The best he could offer was a comforting "shhh" as he rubbed her back. He had endured a lot since opening his eyes, but being unable to comfort the girl was utterly heartbreaking. Twice he opened his mouth to offer some sort of platitude; twice he shut his mouth because he could think of nothing to say. Once again the room won.

Eternity-long minutes later, Siân stopped shaking. Silence hung around them; puffy-eyed and pale, she looked up at him. "Sorry," she said meekly, wiping at her face. At that moment, he could see the child she truly was. A scared, lost kid who just wanted to get home to her parents. The weight of this responsibility was heavy on his heart.

"It's fine," he said. "Sometimes you just have to let it out."

She pulled away from him and continued rubbing her face. He could tell she was battling her emotions and feeling self-conscious about crying in front of – for lack of a better word – a stranger.

"You honestly don't need to say sorry. We're in this together, kid."

She looked at him, her uncertainty clear to see. "What if..." she paused. "What if we never get out?" Another silence drifted between them. Her eyes pleaded for something to hold on to. Underneath the grime and tough attitude, she was still a child. She needed reassurance, even if he didn't believe it himself.

"We will. I don't know how, or when, but I promise you –" he looked her straight in the eyes "-- we are going to get out of here."

"Yeah?" She didn't sound convinced, but he saw some of the steel return to her.

"Yes." His tone was firm and convincing. Putting an arm around her, he pulled her against him. "We are getting out of here, Siân. Trust me."

They stood that way for a few minutes until Grant felt the room change around them. He knew that they had passed whatever test the room had required of them to progress. Looking up he saw there was a door in the wall.

"And we'll start by going through that door there."

Siân gave him a weak smile. His heart broke a little: he didn't know where they were or how they would escape, but he was going to lead the way. He might not know who he was or where he came from, but whilst that presented a whole world of issues, it also allowed him a new canvas to paint himself on. This Grant was a protector. He was a man of his word and he would never break a promise. He would protect this child at all costs. Putting the album under his arm, he took Siân's hand in his. He could feel her warmth and her need for something to look forward to. A blast of colour in the bleak horror they found themselves in.

"Who knows," he said, "there might be food waiting for us."

Siân smiled. "Or at least a shower. You're a nice guy, Grant, but boy do you stink," she chuckled as they walked through the door. The stench hit him, even before the realisation that the room was in total darkness. A moist rotten-meat smell with enough of a hint of toxicity to make his eyes water assaulted Grant. He heard the door slam shut behind them. He felt his pulse quicken at the realisation he was trapped in here. He realised that there would be payment for the feast.

"Grant?" Siân called from in front of him, voice cold with fear. That was when he heard the scuttering in the walls around them. His skin tightened as the hairs on his neck rose. "There's something in here with us." Siân whimpered. He wanted to call out to her-- he had taken his vow to protect the girl to heart-- yet fear froze his tongue. In the thick darkness, he couldn't make out anything.

Something hit the floor to his right with a sickening wet slap. His heart was racing. There was a heavy skitter on the floor. He could almost taste the wrongness of whatever was in here with them.

"Siân – where are you?" he whispered.

"I'm by a wall. I think." Her voice sounded both distant and as though it was coming from right next to him. He put an arm out in search of her, but only encountered empty space. As he began to pull his arm back, something wet and rough licked his palm. Letting out a disgusted scream, he stepped back, pulling his arm to his chest. It knew he was here. He heard its wet skittering run away from him.

"Grant?" Siân whispered.

"I'm okay," he lied. "See if there's a light switch on the wall." Adrenaline pumping, he turned towards the wet dragging noise to his right. He could die any second, but he had to protect the girl. He heard her moving against the wall as he braced himself.

"Come on," he said quietly to the darkness.

There was a throaty growl as the blackness before him shifted, and something seized him and slammed his body to the floor. Despite himself, he screamed. He did his best to push the shape off him. Its sticky body pulsated with a sickly heat. His hands were pushing against a prickly, furred torso; the matted fur felt damp and slimy under his palms, but he was too busy trying to work out where the clicking was coming from to give time over to the revulsion he felt at its touch. The smell of *wrongness* seeping off the thing brought burning bile to his throat. Suddenly, light burst into the room. He instantly wished it had stayed absent: the creature pinning him down defied a description his mind could fully cope it. It was a thing from the darkest of nightmares. Neither spider, slug nor human, but a mix of the three. Twisted humanoid limbs protruded from a slick, slimy torso, the flesh on them rotted and black. The whole structure was held up by four thick black spider-like legs. A human face sat atop the jellied body, with a mouth full of sharp teeth and red sunken eyes that expanded in rage as it spied its prey. As they locked eyes Grant saw raw hunger in the face. It was enjoying playing with its prey. It smirked at him, and grey liquid oozed down from its mouth and down its pale chin. His bladder let go and as a warmth spread in his crotch, the creature opened its jaws, released a deep crackling screech and swung its head downwards.

Instinctively Grant released his grip on its lower torso, realising now how futile that had been. He pulled his arm back as much as he could and punched the smirking face, knocking the beast's head back. He pushed the creature away; as he rose to his feet, it lunged. A clumsy jump to the right bought him a few vital seconds.

Siân was screaming in the background. He couldn't take his focus off the monster, but the creature now turned its attention to the source of the noise. The mouth of the beast began to move, as a single word forced its way out "Girl". It was offensive to listen to it speaking but worse than that, it had Siân in its sights.

"HEY," Grant bellowed. The creature returned its red-eyed hungry gaze to him. He feigned to the right and ran to the left. He allowed himself a split second to look for a weapon or an exit but could see neither. The room had upped the ante.

He returned his gaze to the creature. It was between him and Siân; the poor girl was white and crying. She locked eyes with Grant, then nodded with grim determination.

"Hey, bug face," she shouted at the thing. "Come get me!" Another scream escaped the monster as it skittered towards her with a speed that belied its misshapen form.

"Siân NO!" Grant shouted. He tried to rush towards her and tripped over his own feet. He landed on his side and felt the wind knocked out of his lungs. The creature turned to face him. Its whole body began to shudder and pulsate; thick globules of grey slime fell to the floor, and a muscular pair of humanoid arms burst from its chest. The stench that came from the birth of these limbs mingled with the already cloying stench of the room.

"What the fuck," he cried. Before he could get up off the floor it was on top of him, the new arms scratching his face as its fanged maw snapped at him in a blood frenzy. Instinctively he put his hand out to protect himself.

It was the noise – a gristly wet crunch – that told him that something had gone wrong, and then the pain hit him. He screamed in agony and horror as blood shot out of the remains of his middle three fingers. It had bitten a chunk out of them. Thick hot blood sprayed across the human face as it chewed, its eyes never leaving its prey's.

Grant felt the room swimming before him. "Yum," the monster laughed, before turning its attention back towards the hysterical Siân.

Clutching his mutilated hand, Grant watched helplessly as she was scooped up by the thick muscular arms that had found their purpose. Grant felt a detached burst of pride as the girl kicked and scratched at the thing, her foot connecting with the face that was dripping in blood, *his blood*, but it was not fazed.

"GRANT!" she screamed, but her voice seemed distant.

Wrapping its arms around her tightly, the monster stepped back and rushed at the wall. As the dust and plaster shattered around him, Grant fell backwards. The pain had blown away with the last of his resolve, and unconsciousness claimed him.

BOOK OF SARAH – BOOK FIVE

3rd January

Well, that's the decorations all down from Christmas. The house looks bald and drab now. To be honest, it's the first year we've ever had them up. I think he thought that if he brought some colour into the house it might help lower my stress for Christmas. Either that, or he's done it for the baby. It's still early days, so he's treating me like I'm made of glass. It's been a refreshing change. My guard might not be up as much as usual, but it's still there. A few baubles and a bit of tinsel can't erase years of hurt. It was his first day back at work today so I finally had a chance to pop out and see Grant. It's been too long. Fourteen days the factory has been shut. Three hundred and thirty-six hours I've had Michael by my side. It's the same every year when they shut for the holidays. Two weeks off, unpaid; we always feel the pinch, but it's the lack of a break that gets me every year. As soon as I heard the door click behind him, I let out the breath I'd been holding since he clocked off.

I stood for a moment, thanking the silence. We'd survived without an incident while he was off. I put my hands over the small bump and offered thanks to the Goddesses who watched over this baby. Might sound daft, but the way I see it, God has done me no favours. He's ignored my screams and prayers, turned a blind eye to my bruises and pain. God has left me with a beast: I've come to prefer offering my thanks to a pantheon of Goddesses. They, at least, give me the strength to carry on.

After a few minutes of enjoying nothing and the silence, I felt a small flutter of excitement. I could feel a smile flick at my lips. Glancing at the clock, I saw I still had a couple of hours to kill. I did my chores as quickly as possible and, after a shower, I was ready to head out. Just before Christmas, we'd agreed to meet today at our coffee shop. I was so excited I nearly skipped the whole way there. I arrived first, which I had expected. He wasn't supposed to get here until one and it was only twelve-thirty. I ordered a hot chocolate and got us a seat in the corner. I tried to read the book I'd brought with me in my bag, but no matter how I tried to focus on the words, I couldn't concentrate. I could hear my heart beating over the gentle hum of strangers chatting on their phones or to one another over coffee. I felt like a silly schoolgirl with a crush, but no matter how I chided myself, I couldn't control my growing excitement. I sipped my hot chocolate and waited.

A few minutes after one, he walked in. My heart stopped for a second as our eyes met. My hand instantly went to our baby. We dare not touch in public, but the smiles on both our faces would have told anyone who was interested that we were a couple in love. He tilted his head to the counter and walked over to get our order. There would be a slice of cake, as always.

Returning with a tray and a smile, I finally let myself relax. He was here, I was here. This had already been worth the wait.

"You look radiant," he beamed as he carefully put the tray on the table. I could feel myself blush. "How's the bump?"

"She's good." I rubbed my stomach, a million things going unsaid. "It's really nice to see you".

He smiled a pained smile. He hadn't asked if the baby was his, but he must have known. It would be obvious when she's born, but that was a problem for another day. Not for today. Today was for coffee and cake. He smiled at me as he said lovingly, "You too, Sarah. I've missed you." He reached down and we hugged, just as friends would do in the festive period. I forgot about worrying. To hell with prying eyes. I just hugged my friend, and it was amazing. We broke away, chuckling awkwardly, and sat down.

We spoke about how his Christmas had been; the present he's had from his parents, the meal and everything in between. The time passed in a hurried blur of laughter. After our second coffee, Grant interrupted me talking about a gravy disaster and reached into his satchel. "I can't believe I almost forgot," he chided himself, and pulled out a brightly wrapped gift. "Merry Christmas." He started to blush, "I know we said no presents, but, well, I knew you'd love this." He passed me the present.

I couldn't remember the last time I'd been given a gift. Michael doesn't believe in spending the money anymore. "I don't have anything for you," I whispered, almost ashamed that I hadn't thought this far ahead, concerned that he would find me selfish or self-involved. Instead, he reached out and put his hand on my knee. Warmth radiated from the spot.

How badly I wanted to kiss him right there. We'd already broken some of our unspoken rules. What would be the harm in one more? "I didn't expect one. Honestly, don't worry." He squeezed my knee lightly, an act of love worth a hundred kisses. "Now please, open it. I've waited two weeks to see your face when you see it." He was beaming. Reassured, I turned the gift over in my hands.

It was a book and a thick one at that. The gold paper shone under the light as I peeled away the Sellotape on the back fold. Carefully, I unwrapped the gift and saw the title. *"Women Of Lore and legend: Calleigh."* It was a black, leather-bound volume. The pages were old and yellowed; the title was in elaborate gold print, sunk into the rich leather.

I didn't know what to say. I could smell the history of the pages. I looked at him. "I... Grant... Thank you," I managed. I was practically hugging the book.

"This was exactly the reaction I wanted," he beamed at me. "I remember you mentioning her a while ago when you were reading all the folklore you could get your hands on."

"Not *all* the folklore," I laughed "There's still about three or four books I've not checked out yet."

"I like the *yet* part of that," he teased.

"Honestly, thank you. I love it." I looked down again at the book.

"Look inside," he urged.

Opening the front page of the book, I saw, crudely written in red pen, *£2.50*. Confused I looked at him.

"I did that," he confessed proudly. "This way, when you go home, it looks like it's come from a charity shop. He'll just think it's something you've picked up while you were out." I marvelled at how well he'd planned the gift. Finally, I would have something of him in my home. How long I had wanted that: something to remind me of him, something to help me be strong when my strength wavered.

"Grant. It's perfect." I moved to hug him. I didn't care. The connection in our embrace was electric. It was just a friend, thanking a friend for a Christmas present. Anyone could see the crumpled wrapping paper. We were just two friends sharing a thousand unspoken words in a brief hug. I sat back down and sipped my tepid coffee, trying to control the smile on my face. I glanced at the clock; I would have to leave soon. My smile faded and my stomach fell.

"When are you free next?" I asked, with more urgency than I'd intended.

"Thursday I'm in the library, if you're able to come?"

"I'll be there." I smiled and sipped my lukewarm coffee.

The conversation flowed for another thirty minutes before we had to say our goodbyes. It was getting harder to do each time. I knew that soon there would be a decision to be made. Yet that wasn't for today. Today was for catching up with a friend. For hugging and celebrating. Tomorrow was going to be the day for hard decisions. Not today while the cake was sweet and coffee warm.

All way home I was excited at the prospect of reading my present. I couldn't believe he'd thought to make it look as though it had come from a shop; Michael very rarely expressed any interest in the books I was reading, but as I only had a handful in my possession, he might notice a new one. Even he, however, wouldn't grumble at me spending a couple of pounds on a book. The house felt cold when I got back. It always did. I walked around and turned on the lights and heating. After a few hours with Grant, I always felt trapped in a prison when I returned. I went through the motions for the rest of the evening. After doing the dishes, I passed Michael a can of beer and left him watching football in the living room. I could hear the commentators arguing over something as I put away the dishes. I'd left the book out on the table since I had come in – in plain sight, where it was less likely to attract attention.

To me, it pulsed with warmth and love, the gold lettering brightly calling to me on the cover. Michael had barely glanced at it since he'd come in. He read the title, shook his head and went on complaining about "them cunts in their offices" at work. Sounds like he's had another warning about his temper on the factory floor. This will be his last one I think. Not beating me has been leaving him feeling very frustrated. His temper hasn't changed, he's just not directing it at me anymore. Since he found out about the baby he's nearly been a changed man. He still forces himself on me, but he's always gentle. Clearly just scratching an itch. His fists have never been raised once since I said the words "It's positive". He's still not a nice man. He still curses and drags me down but I think it's so ingrained in our relationship he doesn't even know he's doing it anymore. It's as natural as breathing to him. In a way, I don't mind. At least he's still being the man I know. This is my normal, it's not a fun place to be, but after this long, I don't think the two of us can be any different. I put a hand to my stomach; I could feel the love coming from there already. I know I've got choices to make soon, but for just now, I'll stick with my normal. Today wasn't the day to deal with harsh fists and broken vows. Not when the light bounced off golden letters on an unread book. Tomorrow I can face these choices. For today I'm going to ignore it. I'm almost too scared to do anything else. I settled down at the kitchen table and opened the book. With all my chores done and him watching the TV, I figured an hour to myself wouldn't hurt. I devoured the first three chapters. The Cailleach has always been a deity of interest for me. Since I picked up that first book over a year ago and realised that I could be a strong woman, she's held a level of respect in my heart. A warrior, a goddess and a paragon of vengeance across history. In Scotland, they sometimes call her Beira – Queen of Winter. They say that she helped to build the mountains and that she carries a hammer with her. Some say she's a banshee; others say she's the mother of Gods and Goddesses. I've never been able to find out much more about her. All the things I've read have mentioned that she's a champion of women and lends herself to vengeance. Maybe that's why I'm so drawn to her. I could always use someone willing to bring real vengeance into my life. Some say she's a hag, others say she's beautiful beyond words. A whole book about her is just what I needed. I'm going to really enjoy this. I'm going to write out my favourite bits in here, just in case Michael decides to get rid of all my books again. That way I'll have a reminder.

Grant's always letting me talk to him about these powerful women, listening while I prattle on and on about them. I really love that about him. If I tried to speak to Michael about any of this he'd probably burn me at the stake. I think the idea of any strong woman would terrify him to the absolute core of his person. Maybe I should mention her sometime!

Enough of Michael though. This entry isn't about him. It's about her. The goddess Cailleach. This book's giving me more information in a few chapters than anything I've found out in months. There's this, for one:

As discussed in Chapter One, the history of Cailleach's name is almost prophetic to what is commonly believed to be her own powers. Cailleach has been translated to mean either 'old woman' or 'hag' in modern Irish and Scottish Gaelic. It is derived from the old Gaelic Caillech (translating to veiled one)– which is an adjectival form of caille (translating to ''veil'.) A word which heavily borrows from the Latin pallium (translating to 'woollen cloak''.)

Cailleach is often referred to as Cailleach Bheurra. Shaun Mallorman has attributed the twin meanings of her name to the legendary 'mother goddess' or a 'mother of horned beasts' – which connects to her worshippers' belief in Cailleach's natural powers over creatures that would thrive in the winter months and in darkness. A common theme in both the old Irish and Scottish lore that is associated with Cailleach is her connection to both winter and the wilderness.

A common folk song from 8th century Scotland runs:

"Oh Dark Mother – Cailleach,

Hear us above the winter winds.

Oh Dark Mother – Cailleach,

Mother of Mountains, Ageless Dark Woman.

Oh Cailleach – Goddess of Winter,

Put down wand and begin the spring.

Cailleach – Crone of Wisdom,

Bring forth new life from old.

Cailleach – observer of all,

Heed your child's plea."

She has her own song. It almost sounds like a prayer. There's so much about her that calls to me. I've looked at other goddesses since that haircut, other mystical women from who I can draw strength, but none seem to grab my interest as much as her. I'm still amazed that Grant knew me well enough to get me something like this.

I hugged the book to my chest and allowed my mind to wander. I could almost hear the song in my mind. A simple drum beat, marking the words; a haunting voice, singing to the darkness. It took me a moment to realise that the voice was coming from me.

It wasn't until I heard him shouting to 'shut the fuck up' from the front room that I stopped.

5th January

He nearly hit me today. I got engrossed in the book and lost track of time – something I never do. I just got so wrapped up that it wasn't until I heard the door shut that I realised not only had I not done the tea, but I'd forgotten to run him a bath. I was reading a chapter about the secret life of Cailleach:

"The Cailleach is ever-renewing – having passed through many lifetimes, transforming from old crone to young maiden in a cyclic fashion. She is reputed to have had over two hundred "children" in her lifetimes. These are often the unloved or abused children whose pain calls out to her in the darkness. The act of collecting the child is reflective of her dual nature, for she brings death to those who wrong her child while ensuring lasting life to the child she collects. For a period in the 13th century Scotland, this myth was used by children who wished to scare wayward parents."

I was so lost in a world of myth, a world where someone would hear your pain and save you, that I hadn't noticed the hours passing. I'd never done this before; I have a strict routine that's helped me survive all these years. The path of least resistance, you could say. Yet, despite that, here I was – sitting in the kitchen with nothing cooking on the hob and an empty bathtub upstairs. I could have kicked myself.

He walked into the kitchen, eyes going straight to the oven. I stood up as quick as I could, knocking over the cold cup of coffee I'd also neglected. "Nice afternoon?" he asked me, the rage was dripping from his voice. I dared a glance at him: his eyes were burning with rage, and I started panicking. I tried to apologise, telling him that it was just baby brain. I thought if I brought up the baby it might help to soothe his building rage. Unfortunately, the fires were already kindled.

He started shouting at me, telling me I was 'taking him for a mug'. That when the baby comes, he expects me to run a tight ship. He said I don't respect him as a husband anymore. He kept winding himself up and, despite my constant apologies, he was shaking by the time he'd finished. What had started as a moan turned into him bellowing in my face, his fists clenched and white. He ended up punching the wall on the way upstairs to the bathroom. I'm proud to say I didn't flinch when I hear the crunch of his fist on the cheap plaster wall. I had a realisation while he was roaring in my face.

If he hurts this baby, I'll kill him.

8th January

He's on his final warning at work. What the hell are we going to do if he loses this job? He's blamed the stress of the baby and me – apparently having someone who cooks, cleans and runs around after him non-stop is stressful. I figured something had happened when he didn't come home on time. The Burns might be a lot of things as a couple, but we are in a routine! When six o clock had come and gone I just chalked it up to him going out with the few people who I gathered could tolerate him at work. I figured it might have been a birthday or a leaving party. I put his tea in the oven and let the bath out. I settled down with my book. Just after nine, it happened. He burst in the door tonight, drunk and raving about how the world was out to get him.

I knew well enough to leave him alone, but he couldn't stop shouting at me when he came in.

"You don't know how fucking easy you've got it," he sneered at me. It took all my energy not to laugh. I have it easy? Maybe he'd like to be trapped in the same house, day in, day out, wandering the same rooms until it felt as if he knew every inch of his prison cell. Never knowing what horror lay lurking in the shadows to get him. I think that would be the best punishment for him: see how well *he* copes, stuck in the same set of rooms for years. Too scared to venture beyond the world that's been created for you by someone else. To be cut off from anyone who loved you.

I'd love to see how he'd react to being raped. He couldn't build himself back up again after being violated. Having the core goodness fucked out of him by someone who should protect him. I could feel words bubbling up, but I had to bite them back. The mood he was in, he'd probably have beaten me black and blue. The anger lingered in me though. I could feel it burning my blood, raising every bit of rage that I had thought was long dead. I could see myself lunging for him, biting him, scratching his face, reducing him to a sobbing mess in the corner. It's what he deserved. It's what I deserve.

Instead, I bowed my head and apologised. Thanked him for everything he did. It wasn't till he stormed upstairs that I realised my hands were covering my stomach. I'm only showing a little, but this bump is different from the other pregnancies; this is a child conceived in love, not rape.

I'd prepared myself mentally for him to fuck me. Normally when he gets like this, he'll shove it in my arse dry to make me scream, but he'd passed out on the bed when I went upstairs.

Who knew he could still surprise me after all these years?

10th January

Today is a good day. Not only did I finish my book this morning, but I also got to see Grant in the library for a few hours.

The book's amazing – not only did it go into her history but it spoke of her links with the Wiccan faith and even went into details on how to summon her for strength and vengeance. Maybe next time Michael annoys me I'll summon her to scare the shit out of him. At the very least I'll get a night off! It sounds quite easy, to be honest, even though I'm not a witch:

"Since the Goddess Cailleach is one of cold honesty, before starting your ritual wear something blue. This will encourage you to control your own truth and build a personal reserve through the day. If you plan to summon the Goddess, you must observe the following – cover your altar in the colour yellow. This will symbolise the sun. Place a blue candle for truth in the centre of your space. Beside it a bowl of snow to represent the dark mother's connection to the harshness of winter. As the candle burns and melts the snow, you must recite;

"I access my fear. I feel it grow.

Dark Mother, come to me and allow me to let it go.

I access my rage. The heat of anger melting the snow.

Dark Mother, come to me, and let my enemy reap what they sow."

This must be done until the snow has melted. Once presented with a bowl of ice water, you must mix it with no more than four drops of your own blood. Pour the water over the candle to extinguish the flame. Whilst this is a simple ritual, numerous writings advise against the summoning of Cailleach. It is said that whilst she is a kindly mother to some, once she removes her veil, the truth is too much for some."

It sounds like a good ritual, but where would I even get snow from to summon her? The thoughts of candles and summoning carried me through the cold morning and down wet streets to the library.

Grant was his usual amazing self. It's always a little harder at the library because he's working, but he always makes sure to come over with a cup of coffee from the café in the building and he spends his lunch with me. He was beaming with pride when I regaled him with tales of Cailleach. I must have thanked him a thousand times for the book, and I'll probably thank him a thousand more. It's amazing the difference a heartfelt gift can make. I can't even remember the last time I received one.

As usual, our time together was perfect but too short. It's getting harder and harder to return home. I can feel the walk back taking me longer and longer. My feet dragging a heavy heart back to a cell.

Would it be crazy to suggest running away together? Leave this city and our lives and elope? Become the people we were always meant to be somewhere far away, where that Michael could never find us? I can't stop thinking about the choices ahead. Once I have the baby, would I subject her to the life I've lived? I'm not naïve enough to think a child will change Michael. Not the way his temper is and I don't want my daughter to grow up watching her Mum be ground down. That's not what my daughter deserves.

11th January

I don't know what's happened. I'm so scared. Michael came home from work covered in blood. His knuckles were redraw. It was dark already when he burst in through the door, shouting my name. I felt my heart stop for a second. There was something about his voice that just didn't sound right. I could hear the drink, which I knew was always a bad sign, but there was just something else. Something that even I had never heard before. A slither of fear. I ran into the hallway. He stood in the doorway like a bloodied nightmare brought to life. His uniform was covered in blood and what looked like chunks of something. I think it might have been vomit, but I'm not sure. He was white as a sheet and shaking, and he stank of whiskey.
"Is a bath on?" he shouted, panic and booze mixing to make him sound like an angry child.

As he was five hours late home, there wasn't a bath on. I'd topped it up with warm water for two hours, but got fed up of having to drag myself up and down the stairs so had pulled the plug and let the water drain away. I considered the reprisal from a few days ago as the water swirled down the drain, but I thought I could get away with it this time. I've obviously never been so wrong.

"What's happened?" I nearly screamed when I saw him.

"Never mind what's fucking –"

"What have you done, Michael?"

"Is. There. A. Fucking. Bath. On," he hissed through gritted teeth.

His eyes were wild. Knowing better than to push, I shook my head, I tried to offer his lateness as an excuse, but he was barely listening to me. Instead, he was muttering to himself about them 'having it coming' and at one point he stood in the living room and screamed "FUCKING PETE". Using this as a distraction, I turned and ran upstairs.

As the steam filled the small bathroom, I heard him on the phone downstairs, speaking quickly and frantically. Creeping towards the door, I tried to listen, but the sound of the water filling the bath made it difficult. I glanced at my watch – it was eleven-thirty at night; I couldn't imagine who he could be talking to. I managed to catch a few snippets: 'Had it coming,' 'not my fault,' and the one that made me realise things were not going to go well - 'taught that cunt a lesson.' He gave an address and then there was silence. Like most wives (I'm assuming), I like to think I'm the expert on my husband. Sure I might not know what his favourite colour is or what song reminds him of his childhood. I do however know what food will make him mildly nicer of an evening, or what his preferred hand is for punching me. I can confidently say I know Michael Burns. I've never known him to have any friends to call. Especially this late of an evening. The idea of him phoning someone to offload his anger about "some cunt" scares me more than I can put into words. It means that there is another side to him. A side that I don't know and have never seen. There are people in his life that he feels comfortable enough to show his darkness to.

I've been the 'cunt' he's 'taught a lesson to' so many times that the idea of him doing it to someone else is horrifying. What goes on behind closed doors doesn't affect the outside world, but if he's crossed a line out there, then it's likely to seep into my life here. I was almost dizzy with fear at this point.

I rushed back over to the bath, which was nearly full, and made sure to put a bit of cold in. As much as I'd love to boil him alive, there's a time and a place. This was neither.

He strode into the bathroom full of whiskey and bravado.

Locking eyes with me, he stripped naked. Bruises were forming down his side and on his chest. The blood on his shirt had soaked through and stained his skin pink. I gasped when I saw how much blood was on him. I opened my mouth to speak, reaching out to touch one of the bruises, which was already a deep purple.

"Burn these," he said and threw his clothes unceremoniously at me.

"What's going on, Michael?" I asked in a whisper. I had an idea, but I needed to know. Had he finally crossed the line he's danced so close to over the years? The idea of "home Michael" being out in the real world was a terrible vision.

"Less you know, the better." He sighed deeply as he lowered himself into the water. "But I'm telling ya. Brace your pussy – cause I'm in the mood to fuck." And with that, he leaned back and allowed himself to soak. There was a smirk on his face that as long as I live, I will never be able to erase.

I crept from the bathroom, the incriminating clothes bundled in my shaking hands. I stood for a minute; I could hear him splashing in the water. I hurried downstairs. He'd told me to burn the clothes, but we didn't have a fire in the house and surely me setting clothes on fire in the back would draw attention. I panicked: he would be getting out the bath soon, and if I hadn't followed his orders, he'd be liable to forget himself. I pulled out the largest pan I had, a deep five-litre steel one I used for boiling chicken and making vats of soup, stuffed the clothes in and grabbed some matches from the drawer.

Shakily I lit one and threw it on the clothes, but it went out without so much as a smoulder. I needed something more, something to help get the flames going. Without thinking, I opened the cupboard above the sink, grabbed the half-empty bottle of whiskey he kept there and poured the contents over the clothing. I lit another match and threw it into the pan. This time the clothes went up. I opened a window as they smouldered, thick smoke pouring from the pan. The smell was disgusting but he'd told me to burn them. I offered a silent prayer to Cailleach to give me the strength needed to survive the night. Things had changed and I was being swept along with them. I knew I would need every bit of strength that the goddess had spare to help me stay afloat.

I heard the water flushing from the bath as he got out. I stood watching the smoke creeping out the pan, the flames died down to work their magic on the blood-soaked clothing. The amount of smoke that was billowing from the pan was filling the room so quickly I realised I was struggling to breathe. I opened the back door and was so glad the fire alarm's batteries had died months ago. I'd actually been asking Michael to change them for a few weeks to start getting the house ready for the baby, but right at that moment, I was so glad he'd chosen to ignore me. With the two windows open and the backdoor, the smoke wasn't as thick as before but the smell was everywhere. As the flames were licking the side of the pan, I could hear him coming down the stairs. I stood transfixed by the flames. Their ability to wipe away any signs of guilt, to erase a mistake and leave no trace was fascinating. He was in the hallway, his feet padding against the wooden floor and yet I couldn't avert my gaze. I could see something in the flames. It looked like a face. I squinted, trying to make sense of what I saw.

"*Michael is a bad boy,*" a female voice whispered in my ear. I started and turned in the direction it had come from. There was nobody there. I quickly returned to the pan; the face was gone. There were the flames and the smoke. Was I finally going mad? Was this the thing that finally pushed me over the edge of sanity that I'd danced close to for years? I tried to tell myself that it was just my guilt speaking to me. I was essentially helping to cover whatever Michael had done. I've read enough crime novels over the years to understand that I had just become an "accessory" to whatever Michael had done. Had I said it out loud while the ramifications of Michaels actions were becoming clearer in my mind?

"Fucking stinks in here," Michael said from the doorway as he walked into the kitchen, and I came crashing back to the here and now. He was naked, his hairy body thick with muscle from the years working at the factory. He walked past me to the cupboard and removed a full bottle of whiskey, barely registering the empty bottle next to the pan. His mind was clearly on other matters.

His arms flexed as he cracked the screw cap and drank straight from the bottle. With a satisfied hiss, he turned to me. The smoke from the pan filled the small kitchen, swirling around his thick body. His cock was hard and I could see it twitching ominously. "I'm gonna fuck the shit out of you tonight," he smirked as he took another drink. My hands instinctively went to the bump. I didn't want him anywhere near me, but his eyes betrayed the brutal truth. He'd crossed a line somewhere tonight and, now home, he was ready to cross another. My involvement in the upcoming activities was mandatory without or without my consent. In short, we were back to pre-bump Michael. The reprieve was over. Another swig from the bottle and he placed it on the counter. Without taking his eyes off me, he lowered his hand to his dick, slowly pulled the foreskin back and let out a small moan.

"I need you," he whispered in a sigh of self-pleasure, his hand slowly working his length. "Get on your knees." I knew better than to even pause. I knelt below him. Looking up at him I could feel the ways of my old life returning. The changes in him might have been small, barely enough to register but in this position, I could see him returning. With his hand on the back of my head and his member trying to choke me I could see the new Michael die. He had no remorse about returning. We were back to normal. The rest I watched from outside my body.

12th January

I'm too sore to write much. My body is aching and I can't sit down for very long without a dull ache coming from my arse. He not only abused my mouth and my front, but when he realised that he might be hurting the baby with his deep aggressive thrusts he ordered me on all fours and spent an hour fucking my arse. Just what my piles need.

Business is back to normal.

The whole day he's been on edge. Weekends are never easy because he's home for a solid forty-eight hours, but this time it's different. He's been grumpier than normal today, but considering whatever happened before him coming home last night, it's probably to be expected. After his performance last night, I was expecting his fist at some point today. A punch for burning the toast, or a slap for not putting enough ketchup on his bacon butty, back to the good old days you know? Thankfully he's still controlling himself in that respect, but at every little noise, he's straight to the window. The eggshells I've been walking on all day are still intact.

I spent the better part of my day trying to get the smell of smoke out of the kitchen. I've had the windows open and gone through at least two bottles of bleach wiping the sides and the floors down, but I can still smell it. I helped to cover up a crime. I can't help but think I'm as bad as him. I have an idea of what he's done, but I can't think about it too much or the fear will eat me alive.

I can't even look at him today. Not that he's noticed; he's too busy curtain-twitching. Why do I feel as though we're coming up to an endgame? Like Michael's finally crossed the line to a dark place where I always knew he'd end up, and now all that remains to be seen is whether I go with him or not.

14th January

Whatever Michael did has set him down a road of paranoia. I've been keeping an eye on the news and the local papers for a clue to what happened the other night. He's not been back to work, but he did have the decency to phone in sick. This means, at least, that he's still got a job. It's now been seventy-two hours with him. It's been a very tense three days.

He's been drinking more, only leaving the house is to buy whiskey. In the last three days, he's gone through five bottles. He drinks, he paces the house, he fucks me, he goes back to pacing, back to drinking, back to fucking me. Whatever he's done is clearly eating him up from the inside. That provides me with some small measure of comfort. I hope it devours him whole. I'd probably enjoy it more if I wasn't dealing with my own darkness. I can't get the burning pan out of my head, the smell of the material as it burned away Michael's crime. I did that. I helped to cover up whatever he's done. I've not been able to settle properly since. I've cleaned the kitchen so many times I feel sick when I walk in because of the smell of bleach. And yet I can't stop. I can still smell the burning. Feel the thick smoke washing over me. I had a dream last night that I saw a woman in the smoke. She opened her mouth to say something to me, but I couldn't make it out over the sound of Michael screaming in the background. I was frozen between wanting to turn to see him and needing to see who or what the face was in the smoke. Just as I started to make the words out I woke up. It's rare for me to remember any dreams I have, but this one won't shift.

Is this what it feels like to start losing your mind?

19th January

I've not been sleeping very well lately. I lie there in bed every night, sore from whatever Michael's done to "calm" himself. I can't even think about him at the moment. I'm more worried about the dreams I keep having.

It's the same one pretty much every night. I'm back in the kitchen on the night Michael came home. I've got the large pot on the hob. In a daze, I walk towards the thick black smoke, towards the flames I can see licking the air. I'm calm and I'm terrified. I feel like I'm dragging my feet through mud, delaying the inevitable. I blink and when I open my eyes, *she's* there. The face in the smoke. Old and young in equal measure. Beautiful and horrifying. My eyes are transfixed. She opens her mouth and my heart stops in my chest for a moment at the screams that fill the air. Death screams, pleading cries of mercy, the yells of a thousand broken bones, the gut-wrenching agony of a broken heart. Before I know it, my own scream has joined the choir of agony coming from her mouth. My skin is tight against my whole body. Like my own body is trying to shrink. The noise coming from my mouth is made up of every kick to the gut I've had. It's the backhand slaps, the bites on my shoulders and the cigarette burns that have marked my buttocks. It's for the bowl of muck he forced down me, for each and every pathetic inch of his cock. For a second, I'm free of it. A blessed moment of freedom. But who am I without that fear? I'll never know. I put my shaking hands over my ears to drown it out and stop the madding terror in my brain. There's silence. Quilted comforting muteness. I close my eyes against my better judgement. To block it out. To block *her* out. But I can't. Even through the silence, I can hear her voice. The sentence that is whispered at the back of the screams. *"I hear you."*

That's when I wake up, covered in sweat and tears, my hands protecting the baby. Every night I sit there in the dark. Praying for an escape from this. My fingers trace shapes onto the bump, hoping that she can see them and know her mum loves her. I hope he goes back to work soon. My reserves are running low. His madness is contagious and I'm terrified that I'm catching it.

1st February

He finally went back to work today.

I thought that the day would never come. I have to give him points for being creative: he told them that I'd been put on bed rest because I was having "complications" from the pregnancy and he needed a week to help me. They know all about the miscarriages so despite his being off sick for a week, they gave him ten days' holiday to tide him over and stay at home to look after me. It's a nice gesture from the people upstairs who he's always calling stupid. They probably think it's good to give the dad time to be with his wife. "They deserve this after..." they'll smugly mouth to each other while getting rid of a problem from the factory floor.

His hand was trembling when he dialled the number, though, and his bloodshot eyes flicked around the room, checking the shadows. His voice was full of fake bravado and laddish humour. "Oh you know what these women are like," he said, chuckling on the phone. "She'll be living the life of luxury while I'm running around like a blue-arsed fly." I could tell from his uncomfortable thanks that they had given him some sympathy and that he didn't know what to do with it. After a couple of minutes and a promise to keep in touch with a return date, the call was over. I could have cried right then. He was going to be here. I wasn't going to escape him.

After he'd put the phone down he snatched it up again and listened for a full minute to the dial tone. He was muttering to himself but it was so low I couldn't hear what he was saying. Michael's paranoia seems to have reached a fever pitch lately. He bounces to the window every time he hears a car door shut outside. He always insists the curtains in the whole house stay closed. He spent two whole days drunk, convinced someone was watching the house from the other side of the road. I've been living in shadows and an almost constant state of fear for the last two weeks.

There was a day when he kept going to the phone, picking it up and just listening to the dial tone. Dragging me over, forcing the receiver to my ear and asking me if I could hear any clicks. He stopped washing on his fourth day and only bathed for the first time last night. I still ran a bath every evening for him at the right time; it's so ingrained in me that I did it without even thinking. He just sat in the darkened room, the TV on mute, muttering to himself.

He's kept his word though; he's not hit me once. But as that age-old saying goes, there's more than one way to skin a cat.

With the world around him so clearly spinning beyond his control, he's used me as his anchor. I've been his toy and entertainment while he's been off. Aside from the almost daily marathon sex sessions he's been demanding, which have left me sore and raw in ways I didn't know possible, he's taken to inflicting new forms of pain. All in ways that won't hurt the baby. Most of them involve me on my hands and knees and him stood above me, muttering and stinking, like a mad, filthy, God, doing his best to strike fear into his subjects, spreading his madness and fear to all those around him.

Any thought of feeling like a powerful woman abandons me when he utters the words: "Get in the position." Then whatever implement he has chosen to violate me with will come out. The list of 'toys' now includes a wooden spoon, a fork, a whisk and, when he's not feeling in a creative mood, his trusty belt. He's spanked me so hard I couldn't sit down without crying for a day. He's pinched and bitten and spat on nearly every inch of me, and all the while there's been that constant muttering. There's a hard distance growing in his eyes. I didn't fight back once. Despite how much I wanted to. Oh, what I'd have given to shove a whisk up his arse and ask him to thank me for the pleasure.

No matter what he had planned, he was always aware of the baby (the bump is getting in the way a lot for him). This meant he spent a lot of time exploring a map of different routes to exert his new brand of control and power. He's entered a darkness that has eaten away at the core of who he is and these new activities are his initiation to the club he's joined.

Each time he started a session I'd silently offer a prayer up to Cailleach. I don't know whether or not she can hear me, but I'm beyond praying to God. The God we learn about as children is cruel and silent. He has never been there for me when I've cried out to him; Cailleach at least makes me feel strong. She gives me the power to endure these abuses that Michael doles out. If I need to send my pleas out to someone, let it be a dark mother.

Then came the end of the time off. It was like a switch in his brain had been flicked. He was back to being the old Michael. The muttering stopped, he finally got into one of the baths I'd run for him. He still looked different, I could catch the need in his eyes to scan the room. But if he was putting on a show, it was a good one, and more importantly, he was going back to work. Last night was the first night I've slept soundly. The dream didn't come and I woke up this morning feeling rested. I practically danced downstairs to make his breakfast and get him out the door. The difference a good night's sleep can make!

Now that our version of normal has resumed, I can finally breathe. I can do my best to go back to the life I was living before. And that means getting to see Grant. There are no words to describe how much I've missed his face, his warmth, his lack of expectations from me, his soft touch and gentle kisses. He understands me but doesn't talk down to me, and that's something that I never will get used to but it's fun to learn. These last few weeks have toughened me up more than I would have thought possible. I've survived this long. Now I have a reason to fight for more. Grant's helped me realise that.

I know I need to leave Michael. I know that it's going to come to a point where I need to choose between them and the choice is simple for me. The truth would have come out eventually, I would rather do it on my own terms. I have earned that. I've earned my right to make the choice for me and my daughter. I choose the man who has tried to show me I can be more. The man who wants me to be happy and cares about me as more than his property. I just pray to Cailleach that when the time comes I'll have the strength to do the right thing.

2nd February

I don't know what to write. But I need to write something. These diary entries are my confessional. A chance to get out all the hardship of my life. It helps me stay strong and today I need that more than ever.

I was so ready for the day, the click of the door to show Michael had left. I sat for five minutes just in case he came back for anything. He might be fooling others at work, but I can see he's changed. He's somehow harder. Once it was safe, I did the chores and got myself ready. I could barely contain my smile. I think I actually sang as I mopped the kitchen.

The walk there flew; the air had never smelled so fresh. I'd missed the world more than I knew. I had the silliest urge to run – just run, flat-out, until I couldn't catch my breath. Obviously, I held back. Nobody needs to see a pregnant woman running hysterically down the road.

As soon as I walked into the library, I saw him. He was just standing by the counter, sorting a pile of books. He looked up at the sound of the door clicking shut behind me. My heart nearly burst as Grant's soft brown eyes locked onto me. Then it hit me. I crumpled. Tears fell down my face and I felt the horror of the last twenty days catch up with me. All the invasions. The never-ending muttering. The sense of claustrophobia. Michael in all his horror and glory. Captivity has a scent, and Michael's immersed me in that maddening stench for twenty days. I'd taken four showers since he's gone back to work to try and wash it off me., but at that moment it was all I could smell.

Without missing a beat Grant came around the counter and wrapped his arms around me. He gently held me as I cried into his shoulder for what felt like an eternity. What a sight we must have made. In his embrace, he led me to the office just off the main counter. He motioned to Jean and as the door closed, I could hear her explaining to a concerned patron about pregnancy hormones. Thank you, Jean. There was something in her eye though, I swear I hear her tut, but I think that's just the remnants of Michael's paranoia. He's finally managed to find a way to invade my safe place.

We didn't speak at first, he just pulled me close and let me cry. So close that, for a minute, it felt like we were one person, his strength staunching the flood of my pain. Slowly the tears dried, and I stepped away. I have never felt more embarrassed in my life and let's be honest – considering my life, that's saying something.

He whispered my name as he wiped my face, his brown eyes sparkling with his own unshed tears. Looking into those eyes I knew I had found a home. Michael's eyes are ice-blue and hard – harder now than I've ever seen them. There was never a home in them. What Sarah Mathews thought she saw wasn't a home. It was a prison. Grant's eyes filled me with warmth.

Because he was working our time together had to be short, despite his protests. He wanted to take the rest of the day off, to spend as much of it with me as he could. I won't lie, I wanted that too. I want it more than anything, to just bask in his presence. I knew that I couldn't. It was a dream of another life. I know I'm going to leave Michael, but that would be on my own terms. I'm not getting ahead of myself. I still can't afford to be reckless. Above all of that need to be near him was my will to survive. I had lowered my armour already today and if I'd spent too much time with him, I don't think I could have come back to this house. Instead, I hardened my heart and explained what had happened. I spared him some of the details: some things are just too hard to say and these are my own private horrors and mine alone.

"You need to leave him, Sarah." He sighed when I'd finished. I could see the pain clearly on his face. "We could run away together. He'll never find us."

"He's killed someone, Michael. I don't know who, but he's finally crossed –"

"It'll be you next," he interjected coldly.

"A line. He's losing it. If I try to leave, I don't know what'll happen."

"He'll what – kill you? He's going to kill you if you stay." His tone was set. I could hear the years of frustration coming out. I knew he was right. He was mirroring my thoughts, but damn him for saying it.

"No, he won't kill me if I stay. He certainly won't do anything while I've got this." I rubbed bump for emphasis. My small, beautiful girl, my guardian angel and shield. I needed him to back off a little, I knew that I was going to choose him, but I needed to decide the when and how.

"And what happens when the baby comes? What happens when he looks at it. Ignoring that. What happens when it –"

"She," I said firmly.

"Doesn't sleep through the night? What happens when she won't settle? Do you think he should be around a baby? The man's deranged."

I could feel the air warming between us, the sparks flying and leading us towards a fight.

"Grant," I said softly, placing my hand on his,

"No." He pulled away from me. "We've been doing this for what? Four years now? I think I've been understanding and patient enough. Twenty days, Sarah. TWENTY. DAYS." His voice was rising, "I thought he'd killed you. I've checked the papers. I even went past your house. The curtains were all closed. The place looked deserted. Do you know how many times I nearly just knocked on the door? Or called the police? Let me tell you, it was a lot. The only reason I didn't was for fear of what would happen if you weren't dead." He was nearly shouting. "Do you know what it's like to love someone trapped by a madman?"

A tear fell from his eye; his brief outburst had deflated him. "Every night I go to bed and worry that I might not see you tomorrow. That you'll say or do the wrong thing and that's it. He'll snap your neck. Sometimes I sit and torture myself with what he's doing to you right now. Is he hitting you while I eat my tea? Is he putting a cigarette out on your arm as I watch *Eastenders*?" I covered my arms self-consciously. I had been trained to take a telling off for years, but this was different. There was no malice here, just concern and love. But even so, I could feel the anger growing in me. "It's tearing me apart, Sarah. I'm not sleeping, I'm barely eating. I spend most of my day worrying he'll hurt you or the baby. I just want to take you away from this. To save you."

"You don't need to save me," I whispered.

"What?"

"I'm not some damsel in distress." I slowly started to stand. "I'm not some cause, Grant."

"I never said that."

"I'm not feeding into some fucking saviour complex." I locked my eyes onto his. Oh, those poor sweet eyes. The hurt and confusion were written as clear as a child's book across his face. "You don't have to come and kill the dragon and save the princess. I've been doing this a long fucking time. I'll look after myself."

"And what? Let him beat another baby out of you?" As soon as the words left his mouth you could see the regret. "Oh, God Sarah. I'm sorry –"

"No man is going to hurt my baby." I hissed

"I didn't mean. It was just... I'm just…"

"Goodbye, Grant."

I walked out of the office. Jean eyed me as I exited. There was definitely something there. If I didn't have time for Grant's judgement, I certainly didn't have time for Jean's. Grant came rushing out of the office calling my name. I ignored him and strode to the front doors. I felt his hand grab my shoulder to slow me down.

I spun and slapped him. "By Cailleach, no man will lay a hand on me again Grant," I screamed.

The library froze. Grant froze. My heart froze. He looked so hurt. I had turned into the thing I hate. Instead of talking to him, explaining that I was hurt and scared, that he'd pressed a button in my heart, I had lashed out. I could feel a fresh wave of tears coming on, but I refused to give Jean or the others watching the drama unfold. The satisfaction of the pregnant woman crying. I rushed out of the library into the street. Only then did I let myself cry. Breathing deeply, I did my best to compose myself.

I looked down the street and my heart froze: Michael was standing outside the hardware shop across the road. I blinked twice and he turned and went into the shop.

I don't think he saw me. I ran home as fast as my bloated feet would carry me. Flat out ran. Turns out people do look at a pregnant woman running funnily. Grant, who'd run into the street to try and catch me, called out, but I ignored him.

When I got home my heart was pounding its way out of my chest and breaking into jagged shards that cut into my soul. I felt sick. Questions spun out of control in my mind. Had he seen me? Did he see Grant chasing after me? Why wasn't he at work? I ran to the kitchen sink and vomited. I cleaned myself up and waited. There were still three hours until he was due home.

I tried to busy myself with making the tea, cursing myself for doing all the chores before leaving. My heart was breaking; I'd destroyed the best thing in my life. I needed a distraction but there wasn't one. I did my best to air the house out. After twenty days on lockdown, Michael's stench clung to everything, tainting it with his madness. No matter what I did, however, time crawled by. After what felt like years I heard the click of his key in the lock. He came into the kitchen to find me sitting at the table (trying to look normal.)

"Mmm. Something smells nice," he said and kissed me on the forehead. He never does that. *"He knows"* my mind screamed. "I'm making a roast for you." My voice was shaky. I mentally prayed to Cailleach for strength. "You know, being back at work's probably making you hungry." I tried to smile. If it read false, he never let on.

"Ta love." He lingered, his icy eyes studying me. I felt like an open book. "Bath done?"

"Yeah – all run for you." I could hear my heart beating. He narrowed his eyes a touch before leaning to kiss my cheek. His stubble felt as though it was trying to claw my secrets from my skin.

He turned and left the kitchen. I let out the breath I'd been holding since he'd arrived as I heard him climb the stairs. I sat trying to calm myself until I heard him get in the bath. Best to get back to the normal routine, I told myself. I turned the veg down to low so they would be done when he got out.

Slowly I climbed up the stairs and went into our bedroom to get his clothes for a wash. The bedroom still had faint undertones of that smell. There was a bag at the foot of the bed. I'd not seen him with it in the kitchen so he must have left it in the hallway. In fact, I'd never seen it before. Call it curiosity or just plain nosiness, but I opened it, and my heart froze. Inside were lengths of chain, lengths of rope and a mid-size bone saw.

CHAPTER SIX

Coughing, Grant sat up, trying to recall what had happened. It was only when the memory of the monstrosity resurfaced that the pain exploded in his right arm. The horror he felt at the creature and fear of what Siân might be going through along with the pain he was enduring. With a moan, he looked at the empty space where his hand had been. Blood was blotted on the dirty rags that had been used to bandage the stump. He could almost make out a memory, a male voice. Its owner had used something hot on his fleshy remains to stem the bleeding. The sizzling of his flesh and the roast-pork smell of his flesh being cauterised had caused him to pass out again. *"Not yet,"* the man had whispered. *"She wants to see if you remember to say hello".* His mind went blank after that.

These flashes of what he assumed was a memory chilled him for two reasons. Not only was someone else in here, but also someone had come and done this to him while he had been unconscious. Panic rose in him. Who was this hazy memory talking about? Who did he have to say hello to?

"What the fuck?" he cried, staring at the grimy bandages. He remembered the monster, the pain as Siân had been dragged away. Her screams rose again in his memory, so sharply that he turned his head and vomited. He had gone from having no memories to ones that just caused him agony and confusion. Pain pulsed slowly and deeply in the wound. But this wasn't all. He could feel something else, something deep beneath the pain that was spreading through his body, the slow dull throbbing of failure. He'd failed to protect her. *Again.* He ignored the thought and stood up. After a spell of dizziness, he concentrated on staying on his feet. "Don't you dare pass out again," he ordered himself.

He was still in the room. The single bulb hung from the ceiling, giving off a dirty yellow light. Dust hung in the air; he felt it coating his skin and dry throat. The floor was littered with debris and chunks of plaster. There was a single door on the far wall but, despite his memory of how the beast that had taken Siân, no hole in the wall. There was blood was splattered on the floor and on the wall where the hole should have been: it had dried to a dirty red stain, the ancient floor soaking up the liquid spilt on it. He assumed this meant his visitor has come in after she had been taken. Did the room mend the wall itself or did his visitor have a hand in that as well? The questions running around his head were too large for him to comprehend.

"Siân?" he shouted. He didn't expect a reply and wasn't surprised when there was only silence. He just needed to feel as though he was doing something, anything, to find her. The painful throb of failure was still heavy in his heart.

He walked towards the blood splatter and ran his remaining hand over the wall. The plaster was cool and dry, and he was surprised to see a layer of white dust coating his fingers. It was as if nothing had happened here.

A burning rage built in him. Before Grant was aware of what he was doing, a guttural bellow erupted from his throat and he began to punch and kick at the wall.

He felt no pain, just a white-hot fury as his fist connected with the wall. He wanted to rip the walls down. He wanted to save Siân. And, as his rage began to calm, he realised, coldly, that he wanted to kill whatever had put him in here. He wanted to rip it to pieces with his hand; he wanted to bite it, tear chunks of it loose with his teeth and feel its warm blood splash over him, gulping it down and laughing. He wanted to bask in its pain, show it that it had come after the wrong man.

All the pain he had endured, the failures and the confusion were too much for him. He could feel them all building inside him, threatening to overwhelm him. He screamed at the empty room. "FUCKING COME ON YOU CUNT," he roared, remembering the invisible force that violated him, and the chorus of laughter at his suffering in that room. It only fuelled the murderous intent now growing inside him. "I'm right FUCKING HERE!"

Memories of Siân, trusting him, danced in his mind. The feeling of being important to someone. Being a protector to a girl who needed him. Yet here he stood. A failure. The thought of her suffering because he couldn't save her hurt more than the memories of being violated.

The wall stood and mocked him, and his rage evolved into something else. His stump throbbed; he ignored the pain that was growing under the bandage. "Fucking pussy," he spat into the empty room, as he gave up his assault. He wanted to find the man that had bandaged his arm and torture him for answers. Cut off his fingers one by one until he confided with Grant about whatever these rooms were. He knew something and Grant would get it out of him. Who was "She?" The man clearly knew something about the workings of this place and through blood and pain, Grant planned to get the answers to these questions. He hoped that the man would resist.

With a new and ravenous blood lust, he walked to the single door. Without hesitation, he turned the handle and went through. The rooms had nothing that could scare him now; *he* was the thing that *they* should fear. He had one goal – get the girl. If she wasn't here, he would kill whatever he found, where it stood. The door clicked behind him.

He no longer noticed the interior. Whatever magic operated here had long since lost its wonder for him. His only concern was finding the girl who'd trusted him. He spied another door, directly across from him, and without a pause, he walked across to open it. He almost laughed when the handle refused to turn. He knew the game now.

He turned to face the room, resting his back against the cold door he waited. The game always started like this. He just had to wait for the room to show its hand. "And I'll cut the fucking thing off," he muttered. A small voice in the back of his mind tried to make him aware that he was standing dangerously close to a precipice. If he got too close, the darkness could and would swallow him. This voice knew how close he was to losing the final shreds of his sanity. How thin the line he was close to crossing was. He didn't allow himself to think of that. Considering all he'd been subjected to since he first opened his eyes, a little payback didn't seem too much.

He looked frantically around, his body tense and ready, but all he could see was another empty room. The bulb cast its yellowish glare around him as he slowly counted the seconds. After five minutes he felt the door shake slightly. The rattling sound startled him, making him flinch. He felt his stomach drop at the unexpected sound. The light dimmed slightly as Grant grabbed the handle. He could feel it turning from the other side. "Siân?" he called, banging on the wood. "Siân? Can you hear me?" He tried to turn the handle, but it wouldn't budge. He stepped back and watched as it turned on its own. "Siân? if that's you, bang on the door."

Silence. The bulb dimmed again. Then he heard it: three frantic bangs. Tentatively, he stepped towards the door and put his ear against it. He could hear a voice coming from the other side. It sounded female and in pain. It was her. She was screaming. With renewed vigour, he began to beat at the door. He finally had something to project his rage onto. He used his feet, his good hand and at one point tried to barge in with his shoulder, but still, the door stood. He didn't realise until he stopped, panting and gasping for air, that he'd been screaming the whole time: his throat was raw, his eyes watering. The door, despite his assault, remained unscratched. Uncertain of how to proceed, he put his ear back to the wood but could hear nothing except his heartbeat. Knowing it was useless, but unable to resist, he tried the handle one last time. It didn't move an inch.

She was so close; he could see her smile of relief when he came through the door. Tears began to prickle his eyes, he gently put his remaining hand on the smooth wood. Tentatively hoping that it would be enough to let him through the few inches separating him from his charge. Yet he knew it wouldn't be enough. This place had shown a callous disregard for his feelings at every turn. Love and hope didn't exist in this room, or any of the others he had been through on his own. It was only when he was with Siân that there had been hope. There had been the kindling of love and now here was his punishment for believing there could be more than the off-white walls.

With a defeated sigh, he turned away from the door, ready to play whatever game the room had in store. Grant would crawl across broken glass if necessary to get through to the next room.

He yelped as the room was plunged into total darkness. Ice-cold fear replaced the rage that had been building in him; for all his bravado, Grant suddenly felt sick to his empty stomach. His skin tightened as goosebumps broke out across his whole body, his breath stuck in his throat. He tried to concentrate on his surroundings. The game had begun.

The suffocating silence broke as something skittered across the wooden floor. He knew that sound. Unable to see, he took a step back and nearly screamed when the door handle poked into his spine. The room had felt bigger before the darkness set in. Pushing back against the door, trying to make himself as small as he could, he waited. The noise of the creature moving in the darkness filled the room. He held his breath and tried to pinpoint where it was. Fear gripped him even more tightly when he realised that there was more than one: he could now hear three distinct sets of movements in the darkness around him. Slowly he exhaled, trying to not draw any unnecessary attention to himself. His stump began to burn fiercely. The urge to rip the bandage off, to scratch and pull at the pain, was almost too much to bear. The fiery itch crawled down his arm, leaving a trail of internal fire as it went. He pulled the arm up across his chest and held it with his good hand, hoping to remind it, that this was how an arm should feel.

Something oily and wet scurried against his legs. He held his breath as thick bristles slid past his jeans and into the darkness. Doing his best to ignore the pain pulsating where his hand had been, he tried to get some sort of bearing on the creatures. He could feel thick wetness sticking his jeans to his leg, soaking into his skin. He wasn't surprised to feel a burning sensation; it was easy to ignore compared with what he was feeling in his arm. He wanted to scream from fear and the all-consuming pain erupting from the stump.

"I know you're here," a dark male voice whispered around him. Fear paralysed him. "Grant," it called from the darkness. "I believe you were looking for me." He heard movement around him and pushed himself further into the doorway, trying to take up as little space as possible. "Oh, Grant. This isn't any way to act around another person. Where are your manners?" He licked his lips, ready to call into the darkness.

"What would Siân say? I might need help." The man's tone was almost jovial, but an unmistakable threat crept into the next words. "She certainly does."

Grant remembered the sound of Siân screaming. She was just on the other side of the door. Quietly, he reached down and tried to turn the handle. It didn't budge. He felt like screaming.

The voice didn't stop its taunting. "What would Sarah say?" Grant's heart quickened at the mention of her name. "Imagine what could have happened to her."

With all that had happened, he'd almost forgotten that she was stuck here as well. He'd been so caught up in his own misery and suffering that he had lost sight of his main goal: to get to her. That was two people he'd failed to save if the man was to be believed. He opened his mouth to speak, although whether to offer apologies or beg for information he didn't know. His rage and bloodlust had disappeared so completely he almost forgot his plan to dish out his rage on this man. The chance to speak to his taunter was ripped away from him when a hand shot from the darkness and grabbed him by the throat.

The grip was strong and painful; it was crushing his windpipe. The speed of the attack left him momentarily dazed. He felt himself lifted from the ground.

"You've been a very bad boy Grant," the voice hissed, and his attacker threw him effortlessly across the room. Instinctively putting his hands out to cushion the fall, he realised as his stump smashed into the floor the error he had made. Pain exploded where his hand used to be, and he felt fresh blood soaking through the dirty bandage. Screaming in pain and fighting against passing out, Grant tried to turn to face his attacker, but in the darkness he was blind. Heavy footsteps crossed the room; shuffling away from them, he backed into something moist and prickly. Thick bristles pushed through the dirty fabric of his battered t-shirt.

Groaning with disgust as warm sticky residue soaked through the material and began to burn his skin, Grant tried to push himself away. Suddenly, but not surprisingly, the mass made a clicking noise and sounded like it shuddered towards him. Before it could find him, however, Grant felt hands grab him by the scruff of the t-shirt and haul him to his feet. Swinging blindly with his good hand, he felt his fist connect with something. Weakened as he was, he expected some kind of retaliation, but instead, there was a burst of laughter. "Good! Now you get it," the voice chuckled and drove a fist into his stomach. The punch expelled air from his lungs and he doubled over. Before he could recover his breath, a hand grabbed him roughly by the hair and pulled him back into a standing position.

"Oh, we expected better than this from a big man like you," the voice teased, as it landed a punch on his jaw. His head snapped back as much as the fist in his hair allowed it to. He tasted blood but was beyond feeling any new levels of pain. "A big brute like you and you've barely made it this far."

Grant felt consciousness slipping away. The rage that had burned in him mere minutes before had been extinguished. This was it: the moment that he gave up. But a hard slap brought him back to the suffering. "Oh no you don't," the voice commanded. The mirth was leaving his tone. "You have to *feel* this." Grant felt the rough hands gently tapping at his face. "It's what *she* would want."

"Who?" Grant croaked in the darkness. Instead of an answer the man released his hair and pulled Grant closer to him. They were close enough to embrace, and yet through the darkness, Grant couldn't make out anything about his assailant.

"Her," the voice whispered. "If you don't know who yet, you've not been paying attention." Suddenly he licked Grant's face. "I'm Albert, by the way. Thanks very much for asking." The voice laughed. "You taste of terror." Now his laughter was joined by that other, familiar laughter from a million rooms ago.

Every muscle in Grant's body tightened. He couldn't go through that invasion again. Struggling, he did his best to get away, a small shred of fight returning to him. Despite his struggles, Albert's grip remained firm and unmoving. "She saved me," Albert said with the adoration of the pious, as he delivered a fresh punch to the gut. "I'm a good boy now." Another punch. Grant felt blood fly from his mouth as he coughed in pain. "You, however," said Albert. *Punch.* "Are." *Punch.* "Not." *Punch.* "A good." *Punch* "Boy." Grant felt consciousness ebbing away from him again, but Albert laughed and slapped him across the face. "Oh no," he said. "You have to stay awake. How else are you going to see your present?"

Another hard slap brought Grant fully back to himself. His body was a screaming mass of pain. His stump burned, his gut was on fire and he could feel his jaw swelling. "She said that you needed to see what you've done," Albert laughed as he grabbed Grant's hair again. "I honestly thought you would be tougher than this." Grant's scalp screamed as the grip tightened, pulling strands of hair from the roots, and then Albert was dragging him across the room. Clearly, the darkness didn't bother him as it did Grant. Grant struck weakly at the arm with his good hand; Albert's laughter was the only response. "Nearly time, Grant," he chuckled. "You just wait. She says you have four more rooms to go." Grant fell to the ground as the hand released him. His legs were like jelly and completely useless to him.

Landing in a heap on the floor, he gasped for air. Albert continued laughing. "She said I could leave you a present. So I have. It's more a reminder, really." The laughter abruptly stopped. In the darkness, he had lost the man. "Don't forget who you are." As the lights came back on, burning Grant's eyes with its sudden harsh glare, Albert's booted foot connected squarely with his lower jaw and his head snapped backwards. Blood sprayed in an impressive arc as his eyes rolled back and he fell in the space behind him. He couldn't see fully out of his left eye; the swelling that had already started there was obscuring his sight. He wanted to jump up and face his laughing attacker, but the most he could do was, slowly and shakily, to try and stand up. His mutilated arm hung limply, while the other he held protectively across his stomach. His legs were shaking and he hunched over. The act of standing fully was beyond his strength. He looked at his opponent and wanted to weep.

Standing over six feet five, his attacker sported an almost gargantuan muscular build. Wearing thick black work boots and jeans stretched to capacity by bulging muscles, Albert was a sight to behold. Crude purple and red scars covered his thick chest and arms and wept a thick yellow liquid. Black hair covered his bare chest and shoulders. His large, clenched fists didn't look fully human – the fingers were too long, the knuckles too large. Cold blue eyes were set in the face of a teenage boy. He couldn't be more than eighteen, but the flesh that was stretched across the large head was a patchwork of scars, with a dark red crucifix-shaped birthmark that drew more attention than the rest. It was clear from every inch of the boy's body that he had endured suffering that would break a person, but he wore his scars and mutilations proudly.

Albert started laughing. "You're a mess." He licked the blood off his knuckles. Grant almost wished for the darkness back; the mere sight of Albert was painful to look at. "Who are you?" he managed to ask.

"I told you. I'm Albert." He looked at Grant, the boredom plain to see. "She said you were stupid, but forgetting something *that* quickly?" He mouthed the word 'wow', a smirk creeping across his stretched lips.

"Who's *she*?" Grant sat up slowly. If he could get an answer, any answer, to where he was, why he was here, it might help him endure the suffering.

"Oh, I can't tell you that. It'll ruin the surprise." Albert brought a long claw-like finger to his lips, then mimed locking them and throwing away the key.

"Please. Albert. Help me. You don't have to do this." Grant was as disgusted by the pathetic tone of his own voice as Albert.

"I *want* to, though," Albert said.

A firm silence followed; there was to be no more begging. Albert made sure that if Grant understood nothing else, he understood that. "Your present is behind you, by the way." Icy fingers of fear crept up Grant's body. Whatever this man was giving him as a gift, it wouldn't be something he'd want. "Don't be rude," Albert hissed, stepping forward to seize Grant. The nails of one huge hand dug into Grant's cheeks. Albert forced his head around, making sure his line of vision was directed at the bloody mess crucified on the wall.

In a second that lasted more lifetimes than he would ever live, Grant forgot his own pain. His stump no longer throbbed. His heart forgot to beat. His attacker was forgotten. The dirty white walls of the room disappeared and his breath didn't escape his lungs. All he could see was the present he had been given.

It was the eyes he saw first. The eyes of an innocent child who, despite the circumstances, had trusted him. There was no warmth or hope left in them. There was no *her* any longer, to look at the man who had made a promise to keep her safe. He wished there was an ounce of resentment present in the eyes of the girl he had failed. Even that would have been something. A sign that there was a shred of her left. His mind refused at first to move beyond her eyes, unwilling to register the gash across her face: a diagonal cut that had caused her cheek to hang limply at an angle. He could see her teeth through the incision. Her lips had been sliced into four smaller pieces and coated in brown dried blood. Her hair was matted with blood and grime; he could see insects moving lazily through it, working towards a common focal point: the wooden stake protruding from the centre of her head. He could see something wriggling under the skin just to the right of its entry point. The force that had driven the wood into her skull ensured that her head would never fall forward. Her head would be held upright forever. He could hear himself screaming. Somewhere, he thought he could hear Albert laughing, but he was far away from his body right now.

She was naked, he noticed. Her body was suspended about four feet from the ground; she would have been eye to eye with Albert as he'd worked on her. Her bruised and dirty arms were spread, a metal spike driven through each hand and another through her already blackening feet. He could see, smell and almost taste the pools of blood beneath her. The small right hand he had held mere hours before was still dripping, a slow steady drop falling every few seconds, a maddening sound he knew he would never erase from his mind.

It felt wrong to see her, naked and exposed like this. A girl her age would have been self-conscious about her body; to look upon her like this felt like a further betrayal of her trust. Yet he couldn't stop staring at her. He had to see everything. Every agonizing cut and bruise that had been inflicted. There were three deep gashes across each thigh, followed by a ladder of shallower wounds down each of her legs. Her skin was filthy with dried blood and dirt. There were deep lacerations across her stomach; he thought her intestines were bulging through the wounds, threatening to fall on the floor. None of the horrors performed on the bloody mess that had once been a girl called Siân had been painless. Yet he couldn't stop looking at her eyes. He would have given anything at that moment, Sarah included, to have them look at him once more with the trust and hope they'd had before.

"It's a shame when good girls get used by a bad boy," Albert commented, almost mournfully. "If only you'd been a good boy she wouldn't be in this position."

Adrenaline flooded Grant as he bounced off the floor. Roaring, he charged at the monster before him. Albert clearly hadn't expected such a visceral response to his handiwork; perhaps he'd thought this would break Grant. If so, he was wrong. It had done far worse: it had woken him up.

Before Albert could defend himself, Grant was upon him. He wasted no time with soft blows; the time, if ever there had been one, for those had long passed. Using his battered body he drove Albert into the wall behind them, the force of the assault knocking the air from him. "YOU BASTARD!" Grant screamed and bit down on the scarred face. Blood washed over him as he dug his teeth in and pulled away a chunk of Albert's cheek,

He was no longer the only one screaming. Spitting out the piece of flesh, he redoubled his assault. He noticed with absent interest that the crucifix birthmark was no more. It currently lay on a chewed up piece of flesh on the floor. With his remaining hand, he grabbed hold of Albert's throat, and he drove the elbow of his handless arm into the soft tissue of Albert's nose with a satisfying crunch. Screaming in rage and pain, Albert pushed him away; he was still stronger than Grant, but whatever supernatural strength he possessed was at that moment no match for the grief-fuelled assault.

Unrelenting, Grant bounced back with a head-butt. His former attacker screamed as he staggered backwards. Not giving him a second to recover Grant rained down punches: clenched fist first, stump second. Spit flew from his mouth as he screamed and roared in his pain at the monster below him.

"Guess you didn't like the present?" Albert sneered at him through his bloodied mouth.

Panting, Grant paused for a second, and that was all Albert needed to rush at him. Sidestepping, Grant spun and grabbed hold of his attacker's hair, yanking his head back to expose his neck. He didn't think twice, but sunk his teeth, with an animalistic growl, into Albert's throat just below the Adam's apple. Dragging his mouth to the side, he spat a wet chunk of flesh to the ground. Screaming and grabbing at the new wound, Albert lost sight, for a mere second, of Grant's murderous intent. Now he was the one distracted by pain. With a small step forward Grant was before him, planting a heavy punch into Albert's gut. As the air rushed from him, he leaned forward, and Grant used his good hand to grab hold of his head and drag it down, raising his knee with the boy's face. The rage, the assault, the anger all felt natural to him. He could feel a semblance of who he was before this place returning. The fires that were waking deep within in, felt so familiar that he was certain that he could feel flashes of the man he once was.

But he didn't need to know the man he was: all that mattered was the here and now, which involved retribution and murder at any cost. Siân would be avenged if he had to use his last breath doing it. The killer before him was hunched over on the floor. With a kick to his jaw, Grant knocked Albert onto his back, then drove his heel into the boy's crotch. The scream that followed was like music to his ears. He felt the soft testicles under his foot and ground down, deeper and harder than he thought possible. This monster would pay for what he had done to Siân. She had clearly suffered, and so would he.

Grant dropped to his knees. Albert squirmed underneath him, trying to push him off. Grant swatted his opponent's hands away and used his good arm to push Albert's jaw upwards, exposing his bloodied neck. As he sunk his teeth for a second time into the exposed throat and bit through the flesh, he knew he could never return to normal after this. Blood flooded his mouth as he tore through gristle and muscles. Albert convulsed underneath him. Sinew snapped as Grant brought his head up; blood sprayed from the open wound below. Spitting out the flesh and gristle, he sank his teeth into Albert's neck once more. It was a bloody mass of rawly exposed mess now, yet he didn't stop. He bit and pulled a third time, then a fourth lost to his blood lust and vengeance. Albert's eyes fluttered as blood poured out of his wound and with it, his life.

Still atop his prey, Grant dug his thumb into the boy's eye socket. The violence was a part of him now, and his bloodlust wasn't quite sated. As his thumb burst through the viscous thick muscle with a wet pop, he withdrew it and without thinking licked his hand. The taste that filled his mouth was both disgusting and exhilarating. He punched the face with his remaining hand; the wet thud that filled the room made him smile, so he did it again. Then again. He rained down punches on the face that had sneered about the murder of his companion. Blow after blow. He watched the features turn to mulch; he punched until there was no way for Albert to sneer again.

The body below him was no longer Albert. It was nothing. A bloody abused mess that no longer had a name. It would no longer hurt another person and laugh about it. With a final scream of rage, Grant was spent.

A claustrophobic silence filled the room as Grant slowly stood up. Turning to the body on the wall, he let out a sob. In this isolation, he knew it was safe to succumb to the real emotions he was feeling. The rage had left him and he felt the hollow fingers of grief claw at this heart. He had failed her. He had broken a promise to the only thing in this hell that had tried to save him.

Their time together had been brief, but the bond between them was strong. He stared at her lifeless body, allowing his grief to show him in stark detail the horrors he had allowed Albert to inflicted on her. The state of her body left nothing to the imagination. Every cut and bruise on her was another failure. Another moment of agony she'd endured, that he could have prevented. No amount of rage would ever wash away the atrocities unleashed on the girl.

He walked over to her and, tenderly, drew the spike from her left hand. It was rammed so deeply into the wall that with his one hand it took several minutes before it came free with a meaty pop. He threw it at Albert's body, then repeated the process with her right hand. Now free, both her arms swung limply forward as a wet ripping noise warned of her falling free of the wall. With the weight resting entirely on a single spike, there was a sickening rip as her scalp cracked open. With a heavy thud, she landed in a crumpled heap on the floor.

Sobbing uncontrollably, Grant picked her up. She weighed next to nothing. He cradled her in his arms and slid down to the floor. "I'm sorry. I'm sorry. I'm sorry," he whispered through his tears, rocking backwards and forwards.

He didn't know how long he stayed like that. Time had lost any meaning to him. For one last time, he was with his charge. He ignored how cold she was. His mind shut out the state of the girl in his arms as he rocked her. He may have fallen asleep holding her as the adrenaline washed out of his system. He felt hazy and detached in his own body, unaware of what was happening around him. Time passed, and still, he held her. He had let her go once already, and nothing would be the same again. He held her until he had cried every tear his body held and time stretched to an eternity.

Slowly he returned to himself. He felt the throbbing pain in the stump of his arm first. His mouth tasted of iron and ruined meat. Every muscle in his body was screaming at him as the pins and needles screamed for attention in his crouched limbs. He was vaguely aware of a click as the door on the other side of the room opened. He looked up and saw that he had an exit. There was no joy in knowing he had passed whatever requirements were needed to move on. He debated taking Siân with him but knew it would serve no purpose.

Albert had mentioned he only had four rooms to go until he was at the end. Four rooms until he was either dead himself or free of this hell. Grant was beginning to think it was the former option, which after everything he had endured would come as a relief. *Unless it's four rooms until you find her. Sarah.* Regardless of the outcome, carrying Siân's body wouldn't help him in any way. It was time to say goodbye.

Tenderly he kissed her cheek and laid her on the floor. When he stood, his muscles ached and screamed. He looked down at his one-time companion. She was barely recognisable. He didn't want to leave her like this, naked and exposed. Taking off his t-shirt, he gently placed it over the body. "I'm sorry I failed you, Siân. I made you a promise and I couldn't keep it." He stopped to collect himself before hysteria could take control. "I'm sorry I couldn't get you home."

He had no more tears to cry. Turning away, he walked, slowly, towards the open door, only pausing long enough to spit on Albert's corpse. A juvenile act, he knew, but he had nobody to impress but himself and it felt right. As he walked through the door into the next room he didn't glance back. He thought there could be no horrors left to greet him.

He was wrong

BOOK OF SARAH – BOOK SIX

8th February

I'm home. The last two days have been a blur. My heart is broken. My soul is aching. My sweet baby girl. I thought I knew pain. I thought after all these years with Michael that I was an expert on the deep ache of pain and sorrow that could fill a human soul and allow you to still function.

I was wrong. I have never been so wrong about anything in my life. There are layers to pain and Michael has clearly only peeled the top ones previously. This is the final layer. I'm exposed and raw. There is no Sarah anymore. Just this ache. This fucking ache.

There's a hole in my heart now. A wide gaping wound in my existence that will never heal.

She's gone.

That bastard broke his promise.

Six months he managed to resist. Six months he let me believe that I was safe. All these months of enduring his games and his different approaches to abuse were for nothing. All the silent tears I've shed because of his cruelty were going to be worth it when I got to hold my little girl. He's taken that from me. He's taken everything from me.

I need to write this down. I need to get this pain out of me. I need someone to hold me and tell me that I'm going to get up tomorrow and be okay.

But I'm alone.

He's taken everything from me.

My darling baby girl. My Siân.

Cailleach please give me the strength to wake up tomorrow.

10th February

I don't even remember writing that last entry. I've been pretty spaced since I got out of the hospital. They've got me on some really strong painkillers. Mainly for the broken nose I'm now sporting. The looks they gave me in the hospital as he explained I'd tripped and fallen down the stairs betrayed their real thoughts. They knew what he'd done. The nurse who looked after me in the treatment room came close to offering her truth to me. Her eyes were full of such painful rage and pity for me. It was an almost palpable sensation. I could see it on her lips just before the doctor came in to tell me the news that my baby had not survived the 'fall.'

I could have jumped out of the bed and ripped his throat out when he said that. Not because of what he said, but because he said it to Michael, his eyes full of sorrow, placing a hand on his shoulder and offering his apologies without looking at me once. I could have screamed. I think I might have.

Michael's face drained of colour at the words. I could see his panic when it registered that they were going to have to keep me in overnight. That I would have a chance to speak to someone. But I couldn't even say my name at that moment. If I'd opened my mouth, the pain that would have erupted out of it would have ruined anyone who listened.

He never left my side. He played his part of the dutiful husband well, I'll give him that much. They all thought it was because he was worried about the surgery. I knew the truth. The next day, empty and sore, I discharged myself and went back to the house. He didn't leave me unattended once.

Yesterday was a write-off. I got into bed and slept all day. I've never felt so drained of everything. I thought I knew empty, but it turns out that, once again, there was a whole other level. He knows he's fucked now – he didn't even try and wake me up. He's given me space and can't seem to bring himself to look at me. Even in the hospital, he wouldn't make eye contact. He must know deep down he's gone too far this time. There are medical professionals involved. He caught the look on the nurses faces as they came in to check on me. People know what he's done. Maybe he figures that if he leaves me alone long enough I'll forgive him and we can just go back to normal.

He's wrong.

I wish I'd never looked in that bag. He didn't catch me, but the fear I felt after seeing its contents didn't leave me. I couldn't sleep that night. After the days stuck in the house with him, after the bath and the blood and then worrying that he'd seen me leaving the library, sleep refused to come. I've spent many nights during my marriage unable to sleep, listening to him breathing next to me, worrying about what the next day would bring, but this was a different type of concern. This wasn't the usual worry about a beating. I was genuinely scared for the first time in years. I guess you can get accustomed to beatings and mental warfare. This was the first time I imagined him going too far. I wasn't just afraid for myself, either; I was afraid for Grant, too. Michael was the type that would leave me alive and kill Grant instead. I'm his belonging and he's not the sort of man to share his toys. I knew this when I started whatever I have with Grant. Yet in my stupidity, I pushed it as far out my mind as I could. I knew the rules of the game, but I honestly thought I could get past them. I chided myself all night for the happy future I had painted for myself. A future without Michael.

As the sun lazily lit the bedroom that morning I knew I had to warn Grant. I needed him at that moment more than I needed air. It was another physical ache deep inside me that I knew wouldn't go away, but this one I could relieve. I just needed to swallow my pride, which I'd happily do to have his arms around me again.

We may have fought, but this was as good a reason as any to go break down the barrier between us. Such a stupid fight, but aren't they all?

I had to wait for Michael to leave for work. He seemed to be moving slower than usual. There was a glint of something in his eye the whole time he ate his breakfast. I kept putting it down to my mounting paranoia or his remorse at what he'd done. He didn't say anything to me. Just those eyes. Those horrible cold eyes.

As soon as the door clicked I wanted to run to Grant. Instead, I paced. I walked around and round my prison. With every step, I grew more certain that Michael had decided to harm me or Grant or both of us. I lost count of how many times I went to touch the bump that wasn't there. Each time a wave of heartache so deep I couldn't breathe washed over me. Michael would be proud of how deep the pain I was in had burrowed itself.

After two hours I was finally convinced that it would be safe to leave the house. I dressed quickly and walked to the library. It normally takes me forty minutes to get there, but I did it in twenty-five, my battered body aching with every step. I ignored it. When you're living in a state of constant agony, physical pain is the easiest thing to reject.

As soon as I walked through the doors I knew something was wrong. It was a Tuesday. He should have been working, but he wasn't behind the counter. A woman I didn't recognise was there instead, she smiled a phoney greeting at me as I walked around. I could see her looking at my broken nose and black eye. I realised I hadn't brushed my hair and had odd shoes on. In my hurry to get here I'd forgotten that I looked like I had gone ten rounds with Mike Tyson. I glanced back at her and she threw her fake smile back on.

Panic pawed at my brain; the tears were already building. I did a whole lap of the stacks (it seemed much smaller, somehow) and when I realised that Grant wasn't there I nearly fainted. Had Michael already got to him? Was he dead somewhere because of me? The paranoia was running amok now, in my already delicate brain. I felt a wave of nausea and thought for a second I was going to vomit right there. That's when I saw Jean leaving the office.

In all my years of marriage to Michael, I've become accustomed to the variety of looks people cast towards me. The main one is pity. (*Oh look at that poor thing, their eyes will say.*) Then there's the confused concern (*Why does she stay with him if he's done that to her face?*) There's also the I-don't-see anything glaze over *(If I don't focus on her I can ignore the bruises.)* But the only other person who had looked at me the way Jean was glaring at me now was Michael.

"Sarah," she said.

"Jean, I'm looking for –" I began.

She cut me off. "He's not here," she said, her eyes were blazing with the rage I had convinced myself she didn't feel for me previously. "And personally, I think you should leave him alone." The hairs on the nape of my neck stood on end. "Where is he?" I practically screamed.

"Young lady, your hysterics might work on that naïve young man, but I am going to ask you to contain yourself." She looked at me like I was some venomous snake. "You are *not* the only customer that we deal with here."

I felt the first tear escape. "And here come the waterworks," she tutted. I could see Jean had grown bored of pretending to like me. The look on her face was worth a thousand of the hateful words she wanted to throw at me.

Words jumbled in my mouth; I wanted so badly to say something to her, something hurtful or something pleading, but I couldn't decide which. Instead, I just stood there, frozen. "Please," was all I could whisper.

She made no effort to conceal her distrust for me. "He's having a few personal days," she coolly informed me. "After your last…. performance here, it was suggested that perhaps he should be conducting his private affairs somewhere that was actually private."

And there was the word. *Affair*. Jean had cut through all my romantic notions, my vision of a knight in shining armour saving the damsel in distress: I was an adulterer. Grant was, for lack of a better word, having an affair with a married woman. I struggled to speak. Jean in her pink angora jumper and slacks had done a better job of breaking my heart in a few minutes than Michael had done in ten years of marriage. "Now, I know things are difficult at home, but you've done nothing but drag that poor sweet man down for years now. I've bit my tongue for years as you've worked your way into his life. Do you know how badly you've affected him? If it weren't for me, he'd had crumbled years ago under the weight of your influence." She looked me up and down to ensure I knew, without a doubt where her feelings for me were coming from. "After your last trip here there were complaints. This is a haven for nice people. For people who want to get away from the world for a bit. *You*, bring your theatrics and drama for everyone to see. Tsk. And you had the cheek to bring that poor man into it. I for one will be glad to see him moving on to something away from your reach." She waited a moment to ensure that I had understood her. I could feel the eyes of other patrons on me, judging me. "And for goodness' sake Sarah, you might want to brush your hair next time you leave your hovel." Having said her piece, Jean spun on her comfortable yet stylish shoes and walked away from me, leaving my heart in pieces on the dirty library floor. Could I hate her? I didn't think so. The words were so full of hate towards me, but really, she was protecting her friend. She wasn't exactly wrong. I'd held Grant as a white knight to my life. But I'd never taken the time to think about his life. What it was like when I wasn't there. Was Jean right? Probably. Even the comment about brushing my hair. It's what I should have done. It's what a normal person would have done. I'm not a normal person though.

I don't even remember the walk home. I barely remember cooking the tea. Michael's droning about work seemed to come from far away. I went through the motions. Michael seemed like a distant problem, some annoyance that could be put off for another day.

After I'd done the dishes, I went to bed and cried into my pillow. I've had bones smashed. Flesh burned. I've had my dreams crushed and my hope dashed. All of those were preparing me for this final hurt. First my beautiful Siân. Now my gentle Grant. I truly am alone with my nightmare. Someone has put out the only light of hope in the choppy sea of my life. Now I'm adrift in the darkness of Michael's shadow.

I wonder how many years you can run on empty.

More importantly, is it worth even trying?

11th February

No change. Siân is still dead. Grant has still left me. I've got nothing except the pain inside me. It's eating me alive.

12th February

Siân is still dead. Grant has still left me. I can hear a voice whispering to me in the darkness. She's telling me to be strong. She'll be coming soon. I can't listen to her. The pain won't let me.

13th February

She's still dead. I'm empty. I'm alone. I'm drowning in my despair. All I have is *him*. This is my punishment for not being stronger. For not taking Grant by the hand and running away. My dream family is nothing now. There's just us. Michael and Sarah. Destined to destroy each other. The voice sings to me in the darkness. Her words freeze my heart and make me cry soundless salty tears.

14th February

My baby is still dead. Grant has still left me. But now I am full of white-hot rage that at any minute will consume me. Michael raped me twice tonight after I laughed at the red rose he gave me. I asked if he thought a flower would make up for the baby he took from me. The madness in his eyes burned so brightly as he pushed me to the floor and unleashed a flurry of punches on my face. I swallowed three teeth and nearly choked on the blood coursing down my throat.

He laughed as he flipped me over on the dirty kitchen floor, rough hands pulling my knickers down. When I tried to scream as he shoved it in my arse, he smashed my face into the floor. I lay there dazed thinking it would be over soon.

It wasn't.

My jaw, so swollen and bloody, could barely make the shapes it needed to express the pain I felt as he shoved the rose in my vagina. The thorns scratching and ripping. If I'd had the strength to fight him, that would have been the moment. I could see the knife on the counter. The light shining on the steel, making it glow. It became a holy weapon. My fingers twitched with the need to feel it in my hand. To plunge it deep into him. See how he liked things being shoved cruelly into his body. Like everything else, I let the moment pass.

She whispered sweet words of vengeance to me as he slept. I ignored her as I lay still in the bed, blood trickling from me in places that I've become worryingly accustomed to bleeding from. This is my penance for my weakness. I would suffer it for a thousand years more if I thought it would bring her back to me.

17th February

My jaw isn't broken. But I've not spoken since. There seems to be no point. I have nothing to say.

Siân is still dead. I stopped bleeding today. Or I had done. Until he pushed me to the floor and forced himself into me again, ripping the newly healed flesh. I screamed, but not because of the pain: this is a dance I know and the quickest way to finish is to know the order of the steps.

She's stopped whispering to me in the darkness. I'm almost glad. To survive this, the last thing I need is something giving me hope. This is the house where hope comes to die.

28th February

I have three burns on my left arse cheek from his cigarette because I'd forgotten to make the tea.

A black eye for answering back when I thought I had found my voice again.

There's a patch of hair missing from the back of my head where he dragged me screaming up the stairs because I forgot he took sugar in his coffee. My skin is still tender from where he threw the contents of the cup over me.

My nose hasn't healed properly and I'm still spotting on my underwear.

Siân is still dead.

Grant is still gone.

Cailleach has stopped whispering to me. Nothing he does makes me feel anything. I don't even step out of my body anymore. I *want* to feel the pain. I need to feel something. The void of this grief is consuming me from the inside out.

I wish I was strong enough to kill myself.

14th March

My fingers have finally healed enough for me to write again. I zoned out ironing his work clothes. There was a big burn on his trousers. I thought he was going to use the iron on me but he just pushed me to the floor and stamped on my hand he heard it crack. My pinky hasn't set properly, but at this point, I might as well look as broken as I feel.

I am glad she's come back though. The voice in my dreams. She's helped me through the last few weeks. I'm still empty, but she leads me down to amazing dreams. Me, Grant and Siân doing boring things together; going food shopping, sitting on the bus going somewhere. They're never long dreams, but they are full of love.

Then I wake and remember where I am. Love doesn't live here. It never has. But she shows me what I could have had. I don't know if this is another form of punishment or not. Maybe it's just me cracking up, hearing the voices of a goddess nobody knows about, being shown dreams of 'what if'. They hurt me, they heal me, they confuse me. I can hear her whispering in my ear, but I'm trying to ignore her.

The more I hurt, the more I know I'm alive.

And when I've been hurt enough I will simply give up and my spirit will go to my real family. I'll embrace my lost daughter and be complete once more.

19th March

He has fucked me every single night for the last five days. My body isn't healing the way it used to. My front and back burn and itch. He's been restless and more cruel than normal. I'm not sure if it's because he can see that I'm checking out. He's winning, I guess you could say. I don't think there are any winners in this game we're playing. Just two losers stuck together until one of us is brave enough to do what needs to be done.

He came close three nights ago. He slammed me against the wall because I wouldn't speak, his hand around my throat, pushing the air from me and crushing my windpipe. And I felt exhilarated: finally, he was doing it. He was going to do something I couldn't. I could hear him screaming at me, demanding I say something to him. Tell him 'my fucking secrets' as he so lovingly put it. Just as the world darkened and death's light fingers touched my shoulder he let me go. My body betrayed me and took deep coughing breaths. I've never tasted air so bitter and full of failure in my life. I wish I'd choked on it. I wish I'd had the strength to egg him on at that moment. He was so close to finishing the dance; if I'd given him just a little push I know he would have snapped. But I didn't.

Cailleach whispered in my ear again as I was drifting off to sleep. She showed me images of Shirl and the day I went for a haircut. The strong woman I was on the path to becoming. The images flashed to a mangy dog ripping meat apart. I get the symbolism. It wasn't exactly subtle.

Two nights ago it was a dream of me and Siân, she was a beautiful young woman and we were giggling about boys. I could feel *her* presence in the background, lending me the strength to survive seeing the beauty of a life I would never experience. I woke up with a start, so full of rage that I shoved Michael in his sleep. It was a stupid move, like poking a bear, but I needed to release that anger.

Today, however, I sit here alone. Siân's still dead; no dreams will change that. I thought I saw Grant across the street when I went to look out the window today. My left eye is swollen shut so I'm not sure.

22nd March

I can see properly now. I know what I need to do. Michael needs to pay for his transgressions against me.

Cailleach has taught me strength. Her whispers and dreams have paved a crooked path for my broken mind. She's reminded me of the road I was on. Her whispers in my ear and in my sleep have restored a small part of me.

My daughter may be gone from this world, but that was not my fault. She's shown me that much. Her season has ended but her touch has not. She is hanging on for me. I can feel her growing weaker over the last two days, but as she has faded I've felt my strength return.

I have let two men strip me of my power. Michael with his fists. Grant with his false promises of hope. My unborn daughter paid the ultimate price for this. Grant isn't fully to blame; he was as much a casualty of my pain as I was. Yet I gave him my power all the same.

Michael, on the other hand, is something else. The rotten thread that keeps the story together. I shall make sure, when I cut the hands from his arms and eat his heart, that I praise Cailleach for allowing me the strength to avenge my daughter.

23rd March

Michael gave me a library book today. "The Scarlet Letter". He said I might like it; then he smirked at me and punched me in the face. I felt my nose break (again). I've read it before. The message isn't hidden here. He knows. I was, for a second, impressed that he had managed to find a book to convey his message.

I spun to the counter, reaching for the knife I'd been using to cut his sandwiches for work tomorrow. I could feel it in every fibre of my being: this was the moment. I could plunge it into him and begin the process of vengeance.

But when I turned round to bury it in his chest he'd left the kitchen. I heard the click of the front door closing and for the smallest of seconds, I actually worried that even Michael had left me.

Can't keep a baby, my boyfriend or my husband.

I pushed the thought away. Unlike the other two, he would return. I sat waiting for his return for hours, the knife cleaned and ready in my lap.

24th March

I've not seen Michael in twenty-four hours now. I've only left the kitchen to go to the toilet. I've not let go of the knife yet. I'll be ready for his return. I've not heard her voice, but I know she's with me. Her time of power may have passed, but she's in my heart. I can feel her power linger inside me.

25th March

Siân is still dead. Grant is still gone. Michael has not returned. I checked the bedroom during the small hours. The ropes and chains have gone. We are finally in the end game.
I'm going to make sure that this time the rules are different. This time I'm going to win.

CHAPTER SEVEN

Grant didn't even hear the door close behind him as he took in the scene before him. He was back in the room he'd just left. He struggled to catch his breath as he relived the horror he thought he had left behind. He could see Siân's bloodied feet sticking out from under the now blood-soaked t-shirt. The smell of death and decay hung thickly in the air. He walked over slightly and noticed that the blood was rust-coloured and looked almost dry. Time had clearly passed in the two seconds it had taken to cross the threshold.

The rotted, dirty smell that was assaulting his nose was another reminder of his failure that he didn't need. His Siân was clearly decomposing under the t-shirt. The thought brought a fresh wave of grief to the surface. She'd just been left here; whatever magic controlled this hell couldn't even be bothered to move the girl's body.

Albert's body was also in the same position as before. Grant could still taste his blood and feel it on his face and skin. He would have willingly gone through the entire fight again, just to see the shock on Albert's face when he realised Grant had taken his life.

There was no door. He was again, alone with his failure. He studied the walls again; there was still a dirty blood smear on the wall where Siân had been affixed. The blood had dried, but the markings of her assault were still there in the holes that had been punched into the plaster. His eyes were drawn to the other stains on the floor and wall made when he'd taken her down.

The knowledge that he had some variety of trial to face in the room was exhausting. He was running on fumes now; being back here was dipping into a reserve of fight that had long since dried out. The adrenaline he'd been running on since his scuffle with Albert had worn off. Grief cut deep into him. Slowly his eyes moved back to the shape under the t-shirt on the floor. He knew what was under there and yet he couldn't look away. The stump on his hand throbbed and itched, but it barely registered. He knew he should be in agony- – he *was* in agony – but all his pain was focused on his failure to protect the child dead on the floor before him. The body could heal, but that never would.

"Still feeling guilty eh?" said a familiar voice behind him. "It's amazing the way guilt works, isn't it?"

As Grant turned, time took on a surreal slow-motion quality. First, he noticed the height of the voice's owner of the voice; he had to tilt his head to see the battered, bloody face of Albert.

"Thought you'd killed me, eh?" he said, jovially, as if he hadn't been dead on the floor only moments ago. "I'm afraid not. You're in her domain and I'm her favourite. As if she'd let the likes of you get rid of me. I'm her good boy." He spat on the floor before him. The dry wooden floorboards rapidly absorbed the moisture.

"But..." Grant started. The words jumbled in his throat, unable to find their way out.

Albert smirked and tutted as he slowly moved towards him. "At least you can say you tried. Just chalk this up to yet another failure. You're losing all kinds of things at the moment." He pushed Grant back. "Your hand, your sanity..." He motioned towards Siân's body. "Her."

With that final word, the spell was broken. Grant felt a familiar rage starting to rise inside him. He tried to move but found he couldn't. His legs and feet were frozen on the spot. He tried to pull his foot off the filthy floor, to attack the thing before him, but no matter how he strained he couldn't move his legs. Albert was stood just outside his reach, smirking again.

"How's your hand by the way? Sorry – your lack thereof." With these words, a wave of agony washed down Grant's arm. He cried out and cupped the handless stump to his chest. The rancid smell of infection hit him hard and fast. It was only then that he noticed that things were moving under the bandages. The round bump at the end of the now filthy bandage was pulsating almost. His stomach churned. *Don't do it,* his mind whispered as he started to unwrap the bandage. With each layer he peeled away, the smell grew worse. He closed his eyes and felt a split second of pure relief as the full length of the material fell away. Which was the exact moment he chose to open his eyes again.

As the bandage dropped to the floor he could only stare in silent horror while Albert laughed. The stump of his hand was crawling with fat maggots. White wriggling horrors that were eating away and burying themselves in the now clearly infected stump. Mouth agape, he watched as a fat black fly crawled out of an egg on the side. It buzzed lazily as it used newly-formed wings to drunkenly fly away from the ruins that had been his hand. Grant's stomach churned as hot bile rushed up his throat burning as it streamed out his nose and mouth onto the floorboards. He could hear Albert's malicious laughter in the distance, yet could not avert his eyes from the bloodied stump of his wrist. The pain was intense and all-consuming, a throbbing fire at the base of his arm. All thoughts of Siân left him. All he could focus on was the smell and sight of the maggots and decay.

Using his remaining hand Grant tried desperately to brush off the maggots. He was vaguely aware that he was shouting and moaning, but that wasn't his concern. That was when he realised that they had burrowed deeper than he'd first thought, into his forearm. He watched in horror as wriggling bumps moved down under his skin with incredible speed down towards his elbow. A second wave of nausea hit him and he retched again, although it was little more than bile. His body was empty of anything now.

A hand almost tenderly rubbed his back as the hot stream poured out of him. "I could lie to you, pal," Albert suggested, "and say that everything is going to be all right. That this is the worst it's going to be. Do you want that?"

Grant turned, his eyes unfocused and tear-filled. He wanted to say yes. He wanted a single moment of reprieve from everything, even if it was a lie. He needed a minute to just be okay. Instead, he shook his head. This monster before him would pay for what he'd done to Siân. Grant had come this far without the knowledge that he would be 'okay'; he could go a little further. "No," he spat and forced himself to stand up to his full height. "I don't need your fucking lies." His voice was cold, stripped of anything but hate.

"There he is!" Albert yelled joyously. "I thought we'd lost you for a bit there. Oh, she'll be so happy to know that you're back."

"Who?" he asked, confusion taking away slightly from the rage he was feeding off.

"You don't know?" Albert sounded genuinely shocked before a cold smile spread across his face. "Oh, this just gets better. You've not figured it out yet?" Albert's battered bleeding figure danced a jig of happiness on the spot at this news. He smiled through his broken teeth and pointed at Grant laughing.

"Just fucking tell me!" Grant roared at his tormentor.

"Cailleach," Albert said, with a voice so full of respect that Albert felt a chill of recognisable fear trickle down his back. The name had dislodged a memory from the darkness of his mind. "Ah, I can see it's reminding you of something. How about I add a little context?" He leaned in, his fetid breath warm on Grant's cheek. "It was part of Sarah's final words."

There were no words for what Grant felt. He'd survived countless horrors in this hellish place. His body had been damaged beyond repair; he knew his soul was tainted, and he had felt an indescribable loss upon Siân's death. The grief he felt at her murder had been the closest he had come to giving up, to just sitting on the floor with her body in his arms and waiting for something to come claim him. Yet he hadn't. He had carried on as best he could. Through it all, the knowledge that Sarah, the invisible fabled love he'd been searching for, was waiting for him had given him a strength he hadn't known he'd needed until now. Alberts final statement was the final cruel trick of the rooms. He instantly knew it was true. Sarah was dead. Some hazy memory was forming: there had been rain, and he had watched her die. He could hear the guttural scream of rage and desperation she'd uttered with her dying Breath: *"Say hello to Cailleach for me"* it had been full of pain and lost hope. Much like the scream escaping his lips at that moment. He was no longer in his body. Pain and heartache could no longer reach him; his mind had retreated and broken. He felt himself being led gently towards the door. Albert was talking about his husk, but the words made no sense.

Slowly he opened the door and stood before the darkness that awaited him. There was no room waiting on the other side, just a black void. He could feel a slight breeze coming from it. He could hear the light drip of the occasional maggot falling from his dropped stump. Yet he couldn't move. He just stared into the darkness. He was defeated.

"She said that you're ahead of where you should be, Grant," Albert offered with a solemn smile. "I think that's a little down to me. But I won't make you thank me for that."

When he noticed that Grant was ignoring him, Albert reached out and jabbed at his stump. The sudden flare of pain brought Grant crashing back to the battered prison of his body. "Huh?" he managed.

"I said, this is it. This was the last room. You were going to have to do two more." A twisted smile warped Albert's face "Oh one of them was a real doozy. I mean proper shit-your-pants scary." "Oh."

"But I guess you broke early. Maybe I shouldn't have said her name. That's usually a key for people, but Grant, you're just so much fun to mess with." He squeezed Grant's now bleeding stump again.

Grant moaned in pain, but he couldn't take his eyes from the void. She was dead. Sarah was dead and, somehow, he thought he was the reason. A tear leaked from one eye and worked its way down his face. Albert lunged forward and licked it away. His breath should have revolted Grant, but it barely registered. "Pfft. You're no fun now."

The room slowly darkened and seemed to shift before his eyes. He could almost see past the magic (and that's what he had come to realise it was) that was giving it shape. When the dirty light filled the room again Albert was back to his regular self, all wounds and blood removed from him. He looked as good as new. Grant glanced at another fly wriggling from his stump. Cailleach's magic clearly didn't extend to him there.

"She's asked me to send you in alone." All humour was gone from Albert's voice. "I'll say this, 'cause you've been a good playmate. Don't be scared when you see her." Grant listened to the words coming from his enemy, but they had little in the way of importance to him. He didn't think anything would anymore. There might be answers in that void, but without Sarah, without Siân, they were pointless to him now. He had no reason to make it out of here. The anger, the need to survive, had gone. He was lost in a sea of grief, with only pain as a companion. "She'll explain things to you," Albert said. "This is your chance. Your only chance to atone. Be honest with her and remember your manners."

With that, he pushed Grant into the darkness. The only sound Grant could hear was the click of the door as it locked behind him. He knew, however, that this was it. He had entered the final scenes of the nightmare that had become his life.

BOOK OF SARAH – BOOK SEVEN

March 31st

I had to leave the house today. I needed to get out from inside those walls. It wasn't as easy as I thought it would be to just walk out the door. I nearly had a panic attack when I stepped outside. I'd always thought that Michael had kept me a prisoner, in our home and in our marriage. Now that it's just me and I'm the only one accountable for my own actions, I see that I was keeping myself just as much a prisoner as he did. There were so many chances to break free, but that heavy fear in my heart held me back. Without him in my life, I realised that he's never going to leave me. He's so ingrained into my mind that I don't think I could have ever escaped. I might not have been in the house, I might have fled with Grant, but Michael would always have been there.

I offered a small prayer to Cailleach and composed myself. He was gone, and, as much as I could, I had to at least try and spread what was left of my clipped wings. It might have taken me an hour to get out the front door, but the prayer for strength really did help me. I couldn't stop thinking about her in the forty minutes it took me to walk to Grant's house. The curtains were drawn and the hallway in darkness (I looked through the letterbox.) A pile of letters had spread across the floor, mostly takeaway menus but proof enough that he wasn't home. I wanted so badly to knock on a neighbour's door and ask if they'd seen him, but just the idea of it caused a flutter of panic in my stomach. Instead, I stood outside his house for an hour. I saw his neighbour twitching at the curtains and figured it might be best if I moved on. I could have and would have stood there for hours longer.

It rained on the way back home, a dark heavy burst from above that battered my skin and plastered my hair to my skull. I was so lost in my melancholy that I never sped up my pace and I got drenched through. Forty minutes' walk to Grant's and an hour walk home. By the time I made it through the front door I was shivering. My joints ached; the thought of a hot bath was tempting at that moment but felt like something I'd do for Michael. Instead, I dried myself as best I could, wrapped myself up in four layers of clothing and crawled under the duvet. I'm still there now, I can't say I've warmed up any, but at least I'm not shivering.

It's dark outside and the rain sounds almost hypnotic as it beats against the house. It's a nice reminder that, while I hide in this candlelit cocoon, there's a world outside waiting for me. I think the time has come for me to stop feeling sorry for myself. My husband may be gone, my child may have died and I may not be sure what the future holds, but the point of a cocoon is to emerge as something more powerful and beautiful than you were when you went in. Michael might be living in my thoughts for the rest of my life, but I think I might change the view. Let's see how strong his voice is when I'm trying to silence it with some new form of happiness.

I'm going to read the book Grant got me again. I've thumbed through the pages so many times that it's nearly falling apart, but it's all I've got left of him and the woman I used to be. I just keep hoping that when I finally emerge I'll be strong, like Cailleach.

April 1st

Something awful has happened and I don't know how to begin to deal with it. I have nowhere left to turn except here, this little book with all my thoughts and hopes in it. It's sad, really, that these books that I've written in and disposed of throughout my life are the closest thing I have to a friend.

Michael has been in the house. He left me an 'April Fool' gift. I didn't know it was possible to scream until you faint, but it turns out that you can.

I was asleep and heard a crashing noise downstairs. My heart instantly lurched because, despite what I said earlier, I don't want Michael back, yet, true to his nature, as soon as I felt strong enough to stand on my own he found a way to bring me back down again. Here was me trying to convince myself that he now only lived in my head.

I got out of bed and crept downstairs. The only sound I could hear by that point was my heart beating. I saw a soft light coming from the kitchen and almost screamed. I had a vision of walking into the kitchen to find him sitting there in the candlelight, demanding that we "talk." Now I wish that had been the case. Oh, I wish I could see him sitting at the table, long enough for me to run a knife through his chest and show him how strong a woman I am. But he's stayed true to his nature and stuck to the shadows, using trickery and cruelty.

I walked into the kitchen, but instead of him sitting there, I only saw a brown cardboard box in the middle of the kitchen table. I looked around the room, breath held in my chest; the soft candlelight made monsters out of shadows, but I was alone.

I didn't want to open the box, but at the same time, I almost couldn't wait. There was a letter on top. My hands were shaking so badly that I could barely open the envelope. I wish I hadn't now. I wish I'd run from the house and never looked back. Instead… well, instead I opened it.

He's still alive.

I'll be back later tonite. Tell enyone and I'll kill him.

Be waiting for me.

I felt the room fall away from me. I knew his childish scrawl by sight. And that's when I remembered the box. I didn't want to open it either. It seemed to have almost doubled in size since I'd first seen it, but I knew that was my mind playing tricks on me. I took a deep breath and lifted the lid.

The hand inside was grey and had been severed at the wrist. There was no blood, but the candlelight reached inside the box and I saw his ring glisten. I didn't know what to do, but apparently, my body decided for me. I was only vaguely aware of the scream escaping me: I could hear it but didn't realise it was coming from me. The pain in the sound filled the kitchen and ripped away my strength.

I wasn't aware I'd fainted until I realised I was on the floor. I lay looking at a small crust of bread that had fallen under the table; if I focused on that and only that, I wouldn't have to stand up and deal with the letter and box on my kitchen table.

I know how weak I sound and now, as the darkness is approaching, I wish I'd stood up sooner. Unfortunately, I lay there, letting myself wallow in the misery that Michael had once again inflicted on me. I listened to the rain as it battered the back door, felt the cold seep into my bones and closed my mind off to everything. There was just the crust of bread and me. I imagined what a feast it would look to a small mouse while ignoring the grumble of my stomach telling me how hungry it was. I noticed there was a small fleck of green mould growing on the corner of the bread. I wasn't alone after all: it was me and a few million bacteria. I let my mind wander to the last time I ate toast; how it felt, where I was. Before I could stop myself, I was thinking of cake. Carrot cake. Then I was back to Grant and began to cry again.

"Get up."

I felt rather than heard the command. It reached me in the dark recess I had retreated to inside myself. I tried to retreat further, drew myself in as small as I could, as small as that mouldy scrap of bread. I didn't want to get up. I couldn't deal with it. With the box. With Michael. With Grant. I just couldn't deal with this loss.

"Get up."

I felt myself come back to my body, I registered the pains and aches that had spread through me and moaned a little as I sat up to a chorus of cracks and pops from my bones. The darkness was almost comforting, even though I hadn't wanted to come back. I had to face the fact that I was here.

"Stand."

I knew the voice. It sounds crazy, so crazy in fact that I'm not even sure I believe what I'm telling myself, but I knew it was coming from *her*. From Cailleach. There was a strength and command to the tone that couldn't be ignored. That I *wouldn't* ignore.

I got to my feet. It was a slow, painful process, but once the dizziness had passed I stood and took stock of myself.

He wasn't dead yet. Of course, Michael could be lying. He probably was, but I wouldn't let the grief take over again. It had moved beyond Grant: I loved him, yes, but this was the final dance, that I needed to complete alone. If Michael was telling the truth, I would find Grant and get him the medical attention he deserved. If Michael was lying, as my instincts were telling me, then he would pay. Michael's credit had finally run out and it was beyond time for him to pay his debts. Not just for Grant, or my beloved Siân. This was going to be for me. For Sarah. For every version of her that I have been over the years. For every version of her that I will be.

I decided that I would play along. I carried the box out of the kitchen. A closer look at the hand, with its sickly grey colour and the faint odour coming off it, confirmed that there was no way it could be re-attached to Grant. I put it upstairs – I don't know why there, but I wanted it to be safe. I then folded the letter and put it on top of the box.

"Fight." The voice whispered in my ear as I walked from the bedroom. I nodded in agreement, turned the shower on and let the cold water wash my weakness away.

For too long I've been asleep, and the power I held has been dormant in me. I've survived things that would destroy the man who inflicted them on me. I've had my bones broken and my heart shattered. I've grown life in my body and felt it die. I am the patchwork sum of these experiences and pains. As the cold cut into me, I could feel a new strength growing. Its cold claws ripping away the husks of all the Sarah's I was before tonight. The woman who emerged from that bathroom was not the shadow who had entered.

Now with a purpose and a plan, I got dressed and returned to the kitchen. My movements were swift and fluid. My hair had grown a few inches over the last few months; I pulled what I could into my hand and, without a second's hesitation, cut it off. I wanted nothing for him to grab onto. I let it fall where I stood. I thought back to Shirley, her strength and her advice. As kind as her intention had been, the final word had been wrong. I would not run. Not anymore, the time for that has passed. Now it was time to make my stand. If Michael wanted this marrow, – he would have to fight for it.

I forced myself to eat. Cold beans and a cold tin of pasta parcels. I didn't taste them and was barely aware of doing it, but a warrior needs energy. That's what I am now. Sarah Burns is dead. Truth is, she died a long time ago, I just never knew it. Sarah Mathews is dead, too: I'm something new. I am smarter and stronger than even Michael can guess. I will take great joy in introducing him to the woman he has helped to create.

I left the house; the daylight was already fading but I knew my destination. I was gone for an hour and upon my return, I set out the candles I'd stolen. I'm not proud to admit it, but I knew that our local church would be full of them. I had no lights, and I wanted Michael to see me. I wanted to look him in the eyes as I forced him to explain his actions to me. As each wick caught, I offered a prayer to Cailleach. I thanked her for the strength. I promised her retribution.

It's now ten-thirty and he's not here. I'm sitting at the kitchen table, the warmth from the candles thawing my bones. I can feel the smile on my face. It's not a smile of happiness, and I'm certain that to an outsider I look demented. Maybe I am. Who could blame me?

The knife is sitting on the table in plain sight, but I do not care. Cailleach gives me strength. Let him see the blade. Let him witness my rebirth before he feels my wrath.

My name is Sarah. This is my story, and whether it ends tonight or continues, I won't need to document it anymore. I know who I am now. These books have documented my journey. I have arrived.

Chapter Eight

The darkness around him was almost too much to bear. It felt alive and suffocating, yet despite a small slither of unease, he wasn't afraid of it. He began to step back, intending to lean against the door until his eyes could adjust, but there was nothing behind him. He groped in search of a wall, trying to get some kind of bearings, but his hands floated in space. He turned his head to look behind him, but there was only more thick impenetrable darkness. He was stranded and directionless in the void. His eyes refused to adjust to the blackness, but it was almost comforting. He thought he could hear something in the distance but wasn't sure. He wasn't even certain if he was himself any longer, it felt as if that no longer mattered. He felt no pain in his arm and he no longer felt the heavyweight of fatigue he had been carrying. Even his grief seemed to have left him. Everything felt distant and disconnected here. He was finally out of the room. He had made it to the final leg of his journey. For the first time since opening his eyes, there was nothing. He was as empty as the space he filled. Tentatively he took a step forward. Then another, and another. He was moving towards something: what – or more importantly (if Albert was to be believed), who *she* was – no longer seemed to matter as much as it had a few minutes before.

"Come to me," a voice whispered from the distance. "Find me." He trembled slightly at the raw power he could sense in her voice The tone and way the words affected him and made his flesh break out in goosebumps. His heart sped up in his chest. A voice who had never had its demands not met. It had to be her, the one Albert spoke of so fondly. Cailleach.

Grant almost broke into a run, but he resisted. Part of him knew that this was the final leg of his journey. He wanted to believe that a happy ending awaited him, but he doubted it. Nothing so far had gone his way and optimism wouldn't do him any favours now. He was calm and felt no fear, but he didn't want to veer his behaviour into stupidity. The only thing he had rushed for in here had been Siân, but even then, he hadn't been fast enough. He paused mid-thought, waiting for the grief to resurface, but nothing came.

After a few uncertain steps in what he thought was a forward direction, he realised that he could hear something. He thought he could hear the wet sounds of the creatures that had attacked him, but his eyes couldn't make out any shapes as he continued forward. His certainty that this was the endgame grew. If he was to be attacked by the creatures, then so be it. He would fight them as best he could, simply because that was what his body would tell him to do. He didn't think that would happen; somehow, but however his story was to end, he would have to accept it. His time here had shown him that he was not in control of anything. He walked through the darkness for an uncertain period of time, it could have been minutes or hours. Time felt different here, both solid and elastic. If he was present in his body, he imagined it would be maddening. Every now and then he felt something brush against him. He screamed the first time it happened, more out of shock than any real fear, but when he went to bat away whatever it was, he found only empty space. This didn't surprise him, any more than the absence of walls. He was somewhere other than the rooms. It felt like a place of power, but as his feet carried him forward, he began to wonder, what kind?

"You can do this," he whispered to himself as his nerves began to jangle. His voice filled the void with a boom of sound, and he listened as it echoed back. He realised that he had been ambling forward, barely even considering what was waiting for him at his journey end. The familiar jagged edge of fear was slowly working its way through him; the desire to sit down and wait for whatever was in the darkness was growing stronger and stronger. With each footstep, he moved further away from his former serenity and closer to terror.

As if responding to his emotional shift, something grabbed his foot; he screamed and fell to the ground with a thud. The terror was back and hungry to remind him of its presence. Something wet, large and unseen slithered across his back; his scream grew louder and more intense, and he waited for death. It never came. His screams mocked him as they echoed back from all around him in a maddening chorus.

He tried to crawl but with a missing hand, it proved hard, so instead, he got back to his feet and continued walking. He could hear the faint sound of voices around him, but no matter how much he tried he couldn't make out what they were saying. Straining his ears, he thought he managed to differentiate between two voices, both female. Their words were too quiet to make out, but it sounded like a conversation.

As time passed and uncertain miles were walked, he slowly became accustomed to the thick darkness, he knew that he wasn't alone. Between the voices and the feeling of being watched by hungry eyes, he was slowly losing his grip on his nerves. Since his initial fall, terror had settled firmly in and was determined to remain. Still, he walked on. He knew there would be an endpoint to the walk. He just had to reach it. So, he walked, one uncertain foot in front of the other, batting away fear as much as he could. Occasionally he would feel the brush of something as it slid across his feet; at one point something hard and claw-like grabbed his back and tried to pull him into the darkness. He screamed and pulled forward with all his might as he felt it scratching down his back. He barely registered the pain but could feel the warmth as blood trickled slowly down his clothing. He fell over twice more, the second time, he lay there, willing death to claim him. His resolve had snapped and gone. It was fleeting, to begin with, but despite the need to finish the journey, he was so tired. He had nothing left to draw on. It would be a final cruelty if he never reached her. If he never got the answers he so desperately needed. It almost felt like a fitting end for his time here.

So he lay there. He didn't know if his eyes were open or closed. He might have screamed but he didn't know. Tears may have fallen as memories of Siân danced their way across his battered heart; he couldn't be certain. All he *did* know was that he wasn't walking. He had no more strength. Time didn't matter in this place, so as the minutes became hours, the hours days, he lay still and wished for death. After what could have been a few minutes, hours or days, a voice broke through the darkness around him. *Her* voice. The voice of Cailleach.

"*Would you give up the answers so easily?*" it whispered in his ear. It was so close, so powerful, so *raw*, that he knew he couldn't refuse.

Thus, he continued, he walked, and his feet once again carried him forward. More time passed. He waded through the hours. Creatures slithered and flew by him, and still, Grant shuffled on.

He never thought he'd miss the room and its horrors but now, stranded in the darkness, he wished he were back there. Lost in the only memories he had, he soldiered on. What he would have given for dirty white walls and a single dirty lightbulb.

He was slowly growing accustomed to the noises of his surroundings, the light fingerless grabs that pulled at his skin and on occasion brushed against him. He screamed each time it happened, but still, his feet carried him forward. More than once something pulled him to the ground, and each time he was certain that death was about to arrive, but it never came. He slowly realised that she was simply playing with him. This was part of the game. She wanted to test him a final time. Did he have the resolve, after everything he had faced already to cross the void to her? He no longer stayed down, however. He got up. He took a deep breath. He carried on walking. He held onto the slim determination he had. The direction was meaningless to him now, all he had to go on was a blind faith that whatever had delivered him to this point would want him to make it to the very end. With clenched fists and renewed determination, he sped his pace forward. The woman promised him answers and answers he would get.

When he walked into the door in the darkness, he stood transfixed for a few minutes. It was the same door he'd been using to navigate his way around the rooms. There was nothing special about it, bar the fact that it stood alone, with no wall to support it. A sickly white light outlined it briefly now that he was in its presence. He walked around it in a cautious circle, having learned enough to know that nothing was quite what it seemed, and the door turned with him. As he went left, so too did the door. There wasn't even a frame, just a single wooden door with a metal handle. He knew though, that this was it. His final door. The light that was outlining the haunting shape looked like it likely came from a single bulb.

"Ah fuck it," he whispered to the darkness and himself, then reached forward and turned the handle. The door swung open to reveal the same room he had seen so many times already. Without hesitating, Grant walked through the door, allowing it to click shut behind him.

He was in a large room. The walls were off-white, the paint peeling in various degrees, showing a patchy grey underside. There were no windows, the dirty wooden floor was covered in various bits of debris and rubbish. Leaves, broken glass and wrappers sat forgotten and covered in a thin layer of dirt. A single bare bulb hung casting a dirty hue around the room. A single mahogany dressing table sat in the corner, the light reflecting in the oval mirror sat atop it.

In front of the mirror was a giant of a woman. Grey hair hung lifelessly down her broad back. Grant could not see her face;

when he tried to look in the mirror, the light bounced back and hurt his eyes. The power she exuded filled him with awe and fear. He was here. *She* was here. He licked his chapped lips, ready to speak. But how does one address a Goddess?

"You made it," she said without turning. Her voice scratched at Grant's brain. Images of the monsters he'd faced slithered through his mind. Broken flashes of his dreams, of Sarah, played in his memory. "The damned always seek their retribution." She almost chuckled. "Like a moth to the flame, they come to me." Images of Siân exploded through Grant's head, and he screamed. He could smell the room she died in, feel the warmth of her hug, the ache of her death in his heart. His hands flew protectively to his skull as the woman before him began to turn.

Don't look! Don't look at her! his mind screamed, but his eyes betrayed him. Before he could comprehend the creature standing before him, he was hurled across the room. The weight of his pain did nothing to slow his flight.

"You dare look upon me??" she bellowed. "Abuser!" she spat. "Murderer!" As he lay on the floor, each word struck him with physical pain. Her words cut into his flesh. "Adulterer!" Another invisible strike. He could taste blood in his mouth from a slash that had appeared across his face. "It is time for you to reap, little man."

With a speed he hadn't expected, she rushed across the room, each footstep landing with a pounding *boom* that shook his skull and made his teeth itch. He refused to look at her again; if he looked into her eyes he would never be the same. The power raging from her was enticing and revolting. Seizing him in an iron grip, she hauled him to his feet. Her odour flooded all his senses; he could taste her rage, smell her disgust at him. Her grip did not betray her age; everything about her was as god-like as he had feared.

She dragged him towards the dresser. "Look!" she hissed and turned his head towards the mirror. "You disgust me." Tightening her grip, she grabbed a handful of hair and yanked his head back. "LOOK!" she roared, her voice more animal than human.

Grant looked in the mirror. Cold blue eyes looked back at him from a hard and filthy face.

#

The front door would be too obvious. He knew that. Tonight would only end one way and he didn't want that cunt over the road seeing him go in. Pulling his collar up, he walked briskly around the corner to the entry that ran down the street, looking at the familiar gate. He knew which one was his house. He could have navigated this blind, but he took his time, savouring the anticipation of what was to come.

Her nigger lover had bled out so quickly after he'd chopped his hand off that he'd never had a chance to do much more than rough him up a bit. Oh, he'd had some amazing plans for his revenge on that little jungle monkey. But he'd been too eager. He really did need to watch his temper. He chuckled at the thought. The gate swung open and he strolled through the yard. He could see the faint glow of candlelight through the kitchen window; she was waiting for him. His cock started to twitch. He'd make her beg for her life, then fuck it out of her. He could feel himself start to harden. He'd learned his lesson from the whore he'd killed. Fucking Pete, egging him on to fuck her and then laughing when he couldn't get it up. Neither of them were laughing now. Unlike those two, he knew he wouldn't have to worry about her going missing. Nobody fucking cared about her anyway. Fucking Pete. He hadn't been laughing when Michael had his hands around his throat. Oh, he'd got it up then all right. Like a steel fucking rod – which he'd happily used on the slag. He'd enjoyed Pete's dead eyes watching him bite her, tasting her and then cutting her open. The smile on his face when he left was the closest he'd come to feeling any happiness in years.

By the time he opened the kitchen door his cock was so hard, it was throbbing. He was aching to make her bleed and beg. Just like the old days. Before he got soft and let her walk all over him. Fucking baby. Little nigger thing deserved to get beaten out of her. If it was his, he wouldn't have laid a hand on her. But the thought of that (huge) black cock inside her filled him with disgust. He wouldn't be made a mug of in the hospital when she shat it out of her. Best to take care of things at home. He was the man of the house and he'd let her forget it. But Daddy was home and he had run out of patience.

The kitchen was empty. He had expected to find her sitting at the table. He was almost expecting her to have his tea on the table and a bath run. But he knew that the time for that was long past. There would be no more baths run for him. She needed to be punished. He'd been soft on her and now it was time to pay the price. It had started with that fucking library card. Reading those books had filled her with ideas. Then he let her cut her hair and look like a boy. Oh no. It was time to show her that he was the man. He was stronger than her. He was all she could hope for in this world.

"Sarah!" He shouted to the darkness in the hallway. His voice filled the house. It was glad to have him home.

"I'm right here," she whispered as she stepped out of the doorway.

The candlelight suited her, her features were softened. He realised she'd chopped off her hair again, but in this light it suited her. He was almost struck by how beautiful she was as shadows danced across her face. His cock twitched in

295

appreciation. She wouldn't be beautiful for long. He would see to that.

She was naked. As she strode into the kitchen, he felt, for the first time in years, a flutter of nerves. She was supposed to be afraid of him, shaking and crying and begging for all to be forgiven. The warm light danced on her body. His mouth was dry. He actually felt a cold slither of uncertainty. Why wasn't she shaking? Why wasn't she scared?

"You get my present?" he was aiming for a sneer, but what came out sounded almost pleading.

"Yes." She sounded too calm. "Is he dead?"

"What?" His rage began to burn deeply; after all this time all she could think about was that fucker?

"Is. He. Dead?" Ice dripped from her tone. He couldn't see her face in the shadows.

"Yes," he laughed, full of a bravado he was no longer sure he felt. "Died to give me your pressie." He knew that would cut her deep. Silly bitch, making him feel unsure of himself in his own home. Fucking another man behind his back. He opened his mouth to twist the verbal knife.

She screamed then. A deep, guttural scream. Fear struck him as she rushed forward. With her hands behind her back, he hadn't noticed the knife, but now he saw it as she swung it towards him. This wasn't how he had planned things to go. Not at all. He dodged backwards but was too slow; the knife sliced towards his face and he felt the tip cut through his cheek. Dazed, he took another step back as she swung at him again. Her scream was piercing his brain, but he knew the game now. It might not have started as an even playing field, but he'd fucking show her who was boss.

He grabbed her by the wrist and slammed his hand shut around her thin weak bones. She struggled and he tightened the grip, felt her bones crunching. With a moan, she dropped the knife. He punched her in the face, laughing as she went sprawling across the kitchen.

He'd expected a lot of things – whimpering, pleading, crying – but none of these were happening. Instead, she rolled over and sprung onto her haunches. He froze. He hadn't expected any of this. But he'd be lying if he said he wasn't enjoying it. Pete hadn't put up a fight. The whore hadn't tried too hard to survive. But this cunt – she knew what he was capable of and wasn't willing to back down. He could almost respect that. He'd enjoy watching that look of defiance flutter out of her eyes as he killed her.

"You've taken so much from me." she hissed. Icy fingers seemed to grab at his neck. "My youth." She spat the word. "Three babies." She was slowly getting to her feet. "A genuine love." She rose to her full height, breasts shining with sweat in the

candlelight, head defiantly raised. "But you, Michael, you will have nothing else from me."

Nothing was making sense to him. He wanted to rush her. To shut her filthy whore mouth. He was reaching for the knife in his back pocket. He could see her mouth moving. Chanting and swaying. Whispering words, he didn't understand. Thinking she was a clever cunt. Never should have let her have that fucking library card. That's where this all started. He should have kept her locked in a room, a single room, and see how she coped then. Her eyes bored into him. "I'll fucking kill you!" he roared across the small kitchen.

"Come and give it your best shot. Kill me and you'll have to deal with her!"

He didn't register what she'd said as he strode across the kitchen. Her lips were still moving, the space between them charged and full of power, as he flicked the knife open and thrust it deep into her stomach. He grunted as he pulled it out and shoved it in three more times. He could feel her warm blood splashing against his wrist as he penetrated her.

"Thank you," she whispered and fell to the floor.

Michael stood, frozen. He had killed her. He looked at the puddle of blood seeping out from her. He hadn't expected it to feel like this. He had expected her to just do as she was told. He could feel his heart thudding in his chest. The anger that had been all-

consuming mere minutes ago had already turned into heartbreak.
He had killed her.

Still, she was whispering. Was she speaking to him?

"I'm sorry," he whispered in a childish voice. His rage had
deflated, his bravado blown away at the sight of her clutching her
stomach. Blood poured freely out of her. He could smell it all
around him. He could feel it, sticky on his hands, as the first tears
fell from his eyes. What the fuck had he done?

She was still whispering. He dropped to his knees and put his
arm under her head. Leaning in he put his ear to her mouth to
hear her voice.

"Say hello to Cailleach for me," she whispered coldly into his
ear.

Before he had a chance to register what she'd said, she gripped
his head and pulled it back, exposing his neck. "AVENGE ME
CAILLEACH" she screamed with a pain and fury that he knew
had been building in her since their wedding. He barely
registered her teeth sinking into his throat, but as she tore a
chunk out of his jugular, he spared a thought for the name she
had said. Her final request had not been for herself but for some
woman, he didn't even know. As he felt the cold fingers of death
reaching for him he told himself that this Cailleach to go fuck
herself.

Grant burst into tears. He had known Sarah was dead, but he hadn't wanted to see how it had happened.

"Why?" he sobbed to the faceless creature before him. "Why would you show me this? I loved her!" His body shook with his sobs.

"You've not said hello." she hissed at him as she thrust him towards the mirror. "She told *you,* to say hello to me. Yet all you've done is cry."

He screamed as it fell into place. The blue eyes that were staring back at him, the white face that was covered in the filth of his experience, all contorted in absolute horror. She had damned him. He'd damned himself.

"Even in death, you disrespect her. Maybe next time around you'll remember your manners." Cailleach cackled.

EPILOGUE

The problem with having the best sleep you can remember is when your body decides to wake, you struggle desperately to hold onto the dreams you've been having. He could smell her perfume, feel her heavy breasts against him, her warmth against his naked chest. Her breath was an arousing caress against his neck as she nuzzled close to him, but in addition to her sensuality, she made him feel safe. Sighing, still half-asleep, he moved his arm to touch the woman who was awakening every inch of his body, the feminine shape that meant he was home, safe and loved, but he only touched the air. She was gone. Moaning, he touched the bed, but the sheets were cold and empty. Slowly, he opened his eyes and stared. It took him almost half a minute to realise that he didn't recognise the room.

He sat up, confused at first, then began to feel the first stirrings of panic. He was in a large, dim room. The off-white walls, with their old cracked paint peeling from patchy grey undersides, were dirty and in desperate need of some kind of affection. There were no windows; the only light was a dirty yellow hue and came from a bare bulb hanging from the ceiling, coated in spiderwebs and dust.

The dark wooden floor was covered in leaves, broken glass, wrappers and a thin layer of dirt. Footprints – years old by the look of them – had been trodden into the grime on the boards. Piles of what looked like junk were scattered to one side. He jumped out of the bed, only to find he was naked.

"What the fuck?" he said aloud. He began to shake; goosebumps crawled over his small belly and through the body hair that covered him. Panic had hold of him now: he could feel his heart beating, hard and fast, and covered his genitals with his hands as he tried to take stock of his surroundings. There was a pile of broken bricks and what looked like a smashed chair in one corner, with some kind of blue material folded on top, but he paid it no attention at first until he'd turned a full circle and his eyes lit on it again. Covering himself with something would be better than standing here naked.

Gingerly picking his way across the cold floor, he let out a sigh of relief when he saw there was a wrinkled blue t-shirt on top of the broken bricks. He picked it up and put it on; underneath it was shoes and a dirty pair of trousers. As he hastily dressed, he could feel something heavy in the back trouser pocket. The clothes were a good fit, and now he was dressed he felt less vulnerable. More able to face his surroundings.

How had he got here? He couldn't remember. It was worse than that: he couldn't remember anything. A short, muffled cry of panic escaped him.

Who are you? his mind whispered. *You might die here.* another, quieter, part of him added.

With all his willpower, he calmed himself.

"Start with your name," he whispered aloud. He closed his eyes, tried to recall. He swallowed hard.

"Hi, my name is..." He extended his arm in a mock handshake, hoping that might jog some memory. Only silence greeted him. He covered his face with his hands.

He couldn't remember who he was. He didn't know where he was. In short, he was lost. He took three deep breaths, then slowly lowered his hands and took stock of his surroundings once again, looking for any clue to who or where he was.

The air was stale with an unpleasant undertone that he couldn't place. The room was abandoned and without furniture, aside from a bare, filthy mattress atop a metal bed frame. He spied, with disgust, a grey, moth-bitten sheet in a pile at the bottom of the bed. The warmth he'd felt there now seemed tainted by the sight of the reality. There were no windows, no light switches or plug sockets, in the room, but there were two doors: one in the bare wall to his right, the other in the wall to his left.

"Well," he sighed aloud, "you've established you don't know where the fuck you are."

His chest was tight with fear. He wanted to shout for help, but knew, somehow, that it would be futile. Wherever he was, he was certain that he was alone.

Forcing himself to move, he crossed to the right-hand door, feeling the weight in his back pocket once again. He reached in and found a wallet. It was aged black leather and looked well-loved, with frayed edges and creases that showed its age. There was no money inside no personal photos, but there were a few plastic bank cards. The same name appeared on all of them: *Grant Wilkinson.* He felt something click. He knew the name. "Grant. Grant Wilkinson." His voice was a croak, but he was relieved. It made him feel a little safer. He didn't know how or why he knew it, but this was his wallet. Which meant these must be his clothes.

The thin t-shirt was plain blue, with a dark stain on the front. His first thought was that it was blood, but he pushed the notion as far away as he could. He was having a bad enough day already. This was a problem for another time. The sleeves clung around his biceps; the shirt was tight across the chest.

The trousers were a nondescript pair of jeans. There was dry mud on the bottom and another dark stain around the crotch and knees. No underwear, no socks; he looked at the shoes. The bloodied white trainers were also a perfect fit. No doubt about it: that these were his clothes. He chose not to ask why he'd woken naked, why his clothes were scattered at the base of the bed and likewise refused to even think about the blood on his clothes. He didn't know and, at this moment, didn't want to. Grant Wilkinson had more than enough to work out for the time being.

"Okay, Grant. You know who you are. Now you have to figure out *where* you are" He looked at the two doors. Both were identical: dark mahogany wood, with elaborate silver round handles. They were the only things in the room that looked as though they'd been cared for. Fine dust hung in the air and covered everything in the room, but the doors were spotless. the wood was rich in colour, and even in the dull light from the ceiling, the silver handles shone. Continuing his original path, he crossed to the right-hand door. Rubble and glass crunched underfoot.

The door was plain enough in design. Aside from the craftsmanship on the handle and its cleanliness, there was nothing to make it stand out, still less to help him identify his location. He couldn't help shake the thought that this door didn't belong in such an unloved room. He crossed to the other door and inspected it: it was identical in every way. He shook his head, hoping to loosen a memory or a plan of action, then walked back to the bed, flopped down and put his hands between his dirty palms, overwhelmed.

Hot tears burned his eyes, trickling down his face to stain the floor below. He hadn't intended to give way to his emotions, but it wasn't every day you woke naked in a strange room.

You don't know that for certain though, do you Grant? For all you know, you've lived in this room your whole life. He shook his head. He couldn't explain, even to himself, but knew that wasn't true. The certainty that he'd been beyond this room brought him strength. Wiping his eyes, he stood up. "You're not going to get anywhere crying," he told himself.

He decided to try the doors. They'd probably be locked, but he had to check. He returned to the right-hand door, reached out and took hold of the metal handle.

He released it instantly, with a gasp:

the handle was white-hot. A red mark was already forming on his dirty palm. Another second, and he would have had a serious burn. He put his other hand on the door itself and was shocked by the heat coming through the wood. It felt like the door to Hell.

He decided to try his luck with the second door. Having learned from the first handle, he only tapped his finger on the second one's raised edge. It was unnaturally cold. Confused, he put his hand against the wood. A wave of bitter cold passed through him; he shivered and pulled back.

A choice needed to be made. He could either try his luck on the Hell Door or open the other, to what must be an ice palace. "Let's see what's behind door number 2," he said aloud, without understanding the reference

As if in answer, there was a quiet pop. Spinning around, he stopped halfway through a turn; the right-hand door had disappeared. Where it had been, there was now only a dirty wall. "What the *fuck*?"

He rushed to where the Hell Door had stood. The wall was the same as the others – chipped paint and dirt – and cool to the touch.

He felt that he knew very little, but he was fairly confident that doors didn't just disappear. For now, he pushed the question aside, to join the one about the blood on his clothes. He turned the remaining door. He knew that he had to get out of this room; there might be answers on the other side of the wall.

In eight steps he had crossed the room. He didn't pause as he turned the handle; didn't allow his eyes to focus on what lay ahead as he walked through the door towards what he hoped were answers. In two more steps, he was over the threshold and free of the room, and the door slammed behind him. There was no going back.

Message From The Author

Well, if you've made it this far, I guess you either a. really enjoyed my story or b. hate-read your way through it. (Again – sorry about that vomit scene! It was divisive in the beta reads!) Either way – thank you so much for not only buying my book but reading this far. It's been my dream for years to write a book and what you're holding in your hands is the culmination of that.

There are some people I want to take a minute to thank here for their support over the years. The first is my husband Terry – he's done nothing but give me all the support he has for every short story, every attempt at poetry and a pretty bad first draft of a novel about Gods living in Liverpool. Without his support, you probably wouldn't be holding this book here. He's been nothing but a support system to me over the years and there are no real words I can type that would encapsulate how much I want to thank him.

I also want to thank my mother-in-law Maria. She is, without a doubt, one of the most special people to walk this earth and without her love and support during one of the darkest periods of my life this book would never have happened. Family isn't always blood and Maria has shown me that time and time again. I'm beyond proud and honoured to be a part of her family.

I'd also like to thank my friends who have had to listen to me talk about my dreams of being a writer for so long that they probably tune me out at this point. Yet despite this, they have given me help and support whenever I've been stuck on an idea or struggling with the conviction to get this book finished.

Special thanks also go to Uncle Frank Productions who designed the amazing front cover and gave me more support than I could ever have asked for during the upload process.

And finally – thanks to you for reading this.

If you would like to follow me on social media to see what I'm up to or what's coming next – feel free to find me on:

Instagram: JameseyLefebure

Twitter: JameseyLefebure

Facebook: James Lefebure Writer

Printed in Great Britain
by Amazon

72354588R00176